PRAISE FOR

THE GRIMFAERIE CHRONICLES

"Loved this book, I couldn't put it down!
A great take on the genre, & the main characters are
awesome. Full of action, adventure, & humor, it's a fun
book." RM

"…an interesting story with lots of twists and turns that will
have you flipping pages all night long…" Patricia S

"As always, I expect the fight scenes in Whit's books to be
done well -- but was so pleased to find out how
extraordinarily well done they are!" Joey R

"It's kind of a cross between Batman, Angel and Jim
Butcher's Dresden files –but also so much more. It's well
written, with great characters and is just a fantastic read, full
of action, twists and surprises. It packs a punch and kept me
turning the pages to find out what happened next. It's just
great, well-written fun. Can't wait for more. This would
make a fantastic movie. Hollywood, take note." Simon B

"Hate that I have to wait for the next book in this series. I
especially enjoyed the strong female main character which is
par for the course with this author." Ruth R

"There's probably 20 pages in the entire novel that aren't
action filled. There isn't a single wasted word. Every
movement builds into the next then BOOM, heart racing
action. The tension is high and the pace swift. The characters
are well thought out and easily became friends in my head."
JSH

BY WHIT McCLENDON

EPIC FANTASY

THE FIRE OF THE JIDAAN TRILOGY

MAGE'S BURDEN
GART'S ROAD
A MAGE AWAKENS

THE FORGE BORN DUOLOGY

REYANNA'S PROPHECY
REYANNA'S FIRE

URBAN FANTASY

THE GRIMFAERIE CHRONICLES

GRIM UNDERTAKINGS
A GRIM SITUATION
GRIM OBLIGATIONS

NON-FICTION/INSTRUCTIONAL

THE JADE MOUNTAIN WORKOUT SERIES

SHORT WORKOUTS FOR BEGINNERS
MORE BEGINNER WORKOUTS: THE NEXT STEP
KETTLEBELL TRAINING FOR BEGINNERS

Grim Obligations

The GrimFaerie Chronicles, Book 3

By Whit McClendon

Copyrights

Grim Obligations
The GrimFaerie Chronicles, Book 3

Copyright © 2021 by Whit McClendon

ISBN-13: 978-1-7326300-6-2

Cover Art by: Wicked Smart Designs
Copyediting by: Tara Wood
Published by: Rolling Scroll Publishing, Katy, TX
Website: www.whitmcclendon.com

To join my mailing list to be notified when a new novel is published, go to
http://www.whitmcclendon.com/contact

You can also Like my Facebook page!
http://www.facebook.com/whitmcclendonauthor/

Or Follow me on Instagram!
https://www.instagram.com/whitmccauthor/

Acknowledgements

As of this writing, we're still wearing masks and social distancing due to COVID. You'd think that a two-month shutdown would have helped me write this book, but it did NOT. Instead, I busted tail to keep my school (Jade Mountain Martial Arts) alive, so I put my writing aside. However, my dear friends still supported me, asked how the new book was going, and said that I should get back to it as soon as I could. I'm truly grateful for them all.

Tara is always there with a word of support or a kick in the rear, depending on what's needed. She helped me tidy this thing up, bless her. Kathryn always seems to ask the right questions about story events when I need her to. She's got a little magick in her, I'm sure. Christina's steadfast belief in my writing has meant more to me than she knows. Lorna helped me with some of the Scots, very much appreciated. Larry has always been thoroughly supportive, and I look forward to attending more conventions with him. Special thanks to Dennis L McKiernan, whom I'm lucky to know, for his enthusiasm and writing tips. Having your favorite author say that he loves your books— well, that's just awesome. And thanks to Brian for patiently enduring my daily nonsense. Musician, author, and therapist, he keeps me sane.

~Whit McClendon

Chapter 1

Demons are a real pain in my ass. They can appear out of nowhere, have bad attitudes, and always seem to have a beef with me. Their claws, fangs, and an occasional ability to use magick against me makes things even more difficult when they show up.

The demon that put itself on my schedule that evening was as big as a bull and twice as cranky. It lashed out with one of its enormous pincers, trying to take my leg off at the knee. I dodged it, knowing that the real danger wasn't the giant lobster-claws the scorpion-thing was sporting, but the stinger. It snapped its other claw at me and I danced out of its reach again, keeping an eye out for the spiky ball that sprouted at the end of its whippy, segmented tail. One stinger wasn't enough, nooo, its tail looked like a damned medieval morning star.

The enormous parking lot of Katy's Legacy Stadium sat empty at that time of night, and for that I was thankful. I had heard that many in the community had opposed its construction—expensive as hell and situated as it was right next door to the existing stadium, but whatever. I never understood the town's fascination with that particular sport, but I was used to more bloody types of competition. Why a demon would appear there, though, was beyond me. I'd have to think about that later; for now, I needed to stay focused.

The demon chittered at me and twitched. It wasn't much of a hint, but I dove aside, and its spiny wrecking ball of a tail smashed into the pavement where I'd just been standing. I got to my feet and watched it retract its weapon, leaving a steaming hole in the concrete.

Acid.

A greenish liquid dripped from the tips of its spikes to spatter on the pavement below. It left tiny hissing potholes wherever it touched. I shook my head and sighed. *I really don't need this tonight.* Even as I complained, I felt a grin appear on my face as if by magick, and I knew I was lying to myself. I was loving this. I needed the exercise.

I'm Kane. I'm a GrimFaerie. To you, I look like an unremarkable human, maybe mid-thirties, brownish hair, not a guy you'd remember. That's just the way I want it. I keep my true self hidden under a veil, an illusion. My actual appearance would creep you out big time. My skin is so blue it's almost black, which is great for hiding in the shadows. That's not a big deal, I've seen humans of every shade walking around these days. However, the fangs, claws, and silvery eyes are what send folks running. I take care to hide my aura as well, for unchecked, its unseen energy causes humans to feel. . .uneasy. When most normal humans see me in my true state, especially if they see me while I'm working, they say their nightmares never go away.

This is why I keep my true self hidden when I'm among humans. As an assassin, I find it's hard to get close to my targets if people are screaming in fear all around me. Don't worry, I'm a good guy. Mostly. I only kill what or whom the Goddess tells me to kill. Demons or evil and dangerous humans often make the list. If some dumbass starts using magick to hurt people, you can bet I'll end up coming for them in the night. And I won't be leaving a coin under their pillow. I'm not that kind of Faerie.

I used the vast parking lot as a shortcut to a Mexican market on Franz Road. I'd made it halfway across when a vertical line of wavering scarlet energy appeared in the air nearby, emitting a foul, sulfurous stench. I recognized the smell right away. The crack between worlds opened wide, and a scorpion-demon had scuttled through, looking pretty eager to make my acquaintance. The rift closed up behind it and the fight was on.

All in all, a pretty ordinary Tuesday for me. As I dodged and weaved, I felt a bit of gratitude that it had been only one vicious, deadly scorpion-demon, rather than three. Or five. That kind of party would have been a lot more work. Only one demon? Not that bad.

In the distance, I spotted one of the town's white police vehicles, striped with red and blue. It slowed to a stop in the middle of Katy-Fort Bend Road, then accelerated as it moved towards a turning lane that would bring it closer to our parking lot. *Dammit,* I thought. I didn't want some unsuspecting cop getting hurt, and I certainly didn't need them to call backup and turn my impromptu exercise session into some kind of circus. I ducked another swipe of the thing's tail and sprinted away from it. I only needed a second or two to cast a glamour but having a scorpion-demon right in my face made that difficult.

The police car turned into one of the driveways that led into the parking lot and the driver got out. My Fae eyesight was far better than his in the dark, and I saw the cop squinting in our general direction. He reached into his car and switched on the spotlight, sending a glaring circle of illumination crawling across the pavement in search of us.

A small glamour is a trifling thing for a GrimFaerie. It's an easy spell to cast, and I've been throwing illusions like that for centuries. Even so, the distance to the officer made it a bit tricky. Were I so inclined, I could cast a bigger illusion that covered the entire stadium, deceiving anyone who looked at it. However, something that big would wring me out from exhaustion. Fortunately, nothing so elaborate was necessary—I only needed to hide myself and my playmate from the cop's eyes. I narrowed my focus and concentrated before flicking a bolt of magick his way. I saw him blink when it hit him, and he shook his head briefly before moving the spotlight again. He got lucky and panned the beam right across the scorpion-demon's chitinous hide.

I sighed in relief as the spotlight kept roving across the lot and back over the stadium's buildings behind me. That moment of distraction cost me. One of the demon's pincers ripped a gash in my left arm, and I sucked a breath in between my clenched teeth. Scorpy chittered at me in triumph. It was smart enough to know it had hurt me but dumb enough to think it mattered.

Okay, maybe it mattered a little. I growled as I dodged the next swing of its claws. I juked left, and jumped away from its tail, clutching my wounded arm. I heal quickly, but man, that hurt. I glanced over at the cop and grunted in frustration as I saw him unlock the gate so he could drive his squad car into the parking lot. He wanted a closer look. Just being thorough, I guess.

If he got too close, the scorpion-thing would kill him without a second thought. I had to take our little party somewhere free of prying eyes, and in a hurry. I figured the next best place for us to fight would be inside the empty stadium. Its high walls would hide us from view from all directions and would at least present a good surface to play on. Fight on. Same thing.

I feinted a couple of times towards the demon, making sure it kept its attention on me and not the cop, and I winced and grabbed my knee for effect. The scorpion hissed as it lunged again with its pincers. I ducked back out of its range, trying to look like I was stumbling, and I turned and bolted for the north side of the stadium, affecting a limp the whole way. That's not as easy as it sounds, let me tell you.

More hissing erupted behind me and I heard the beast skitter across the pavement. It hastened to chase me, under the impression I was grievously wounded. Predators are like that. They prey on weakness.

Good. I don't much care for most humans, but cops generally mean well. I didn't want this one to become scorpion food. I kept limping as best I could until I reached the tall wrought iron fence that bordered the stadium behind the northern end of the field. Beyond that boundary, I could see the yellow pipes that formed a sort of 'Y' shape, sticking up into the sky. I knew they were a target, a goal for the game of football. *Hmph. Silly humans.*

I vaulted the barrier, landing somewhat awkwardly for the scorpion's benefit, then scrambled away from the fence just as the creature hit it. The slender iron posts bent into crazy shapes as the demon smashed into them, opening up a hole large enough to drive a small truck through, admitting the creature to the playing arena.

Still staggering, I hustled onto the wide-open field. It was marked at intervals with sharp white lines and huge numbers. The grass felt strange to me and I realized that it was real-looking artificial turf. I'd have preferred to have true earth beneath me so I could feel its power, but I had to admit that the consistency of the surface felt kind of nice.

I stopped in the center of the field and abandoned my pretense of injury as I turned to face the onrushing demon. I snarled as I bared my fangs, and my arms stretched wide to welcome the demon with my claws. I'd fought countless creatures far more dangerous than this. Hell, I'd even endured a brief stint as a Fae gladiator in arena combat a few centuries back. They'd thrown some horrific things at me back then. I killed them all. Fastening my silvery gaze on the approaching demon, I leaned forward and bellowed an ancient war cry of the Fae. I was feeling macho. I couldn't help it.

The scorpion didn't slow down. The instant it was close enough, it lashed out with its pincers again, each trying to either snap me in half or line me up for another overhead smash from its tail. *Not today, Scorpy.*

I lured it forward, dodging a couple of vicious swipes of those huge claws as I gauged its timing. Once I had the feel of it, I shrugged to my right, eliciting an instantaneous response. That claw lashed out at me, but I was already in motion to my left. I had a plan.

The demon's carapace was thick chitin, its legs and joints sturdy and armored, too strong for me to break. Its impressively mobile and accurate tail also concerned me. I'd seen its range, and I knew that I either had to be well out of its reach, or up too close for it to hit me. There was only one place I'd be safe, and I went for it.

As I skipped around the creature's right side, it turned to face me again, its legs churning furiously to reorient it. When a gap appeared between two of its legs, I darted through and slid underneath the creature, digging the claws of both hands into its unprotected belly.

It did not like that. Not one bit.

The creature freaked. It thrashed as though electrocuted, and it took most of my strength just to hang on while it bucked and danced. It slammed its body down on the turf a few times, knocking the wind out of me, but I took the impact on my back and shoulders to protect my head. Digging in harder with the claws on my left hand, I started ripping and tearing with my right, digging past the initial layer of thinner armor. It didn't take long for me to get to the squishy parts. Once I'd made a hole big enough for me to shove my arm through, I reached inside and went to work.

I didn't know much about scorpion anatomy, but I do know that the good stuff is probably in the middle somewhere. I found a bulgy, less squishy thing and figured it was important. I clawed the hell out of it and was instantly rewarded. The huge arachnoid convulsed and collapsed on top of me. All fifteen hundred pounds of it pressed down, squeezing the breath out of my lungs and making my head feel like it might explode. *Not good.* It pinned me there, and as distasteful as the idea was, I knew what I was going to have to do if I wanted to escape.

Although most of me was trapped, my right arm was still up inside the scorpion's body, and I could move it. Using my elbow to bash downward, I widened the hole I'd made in its underbelly and worked myself towards it. I turned to one side and stole as deep a breath as I could, then plunged my head up inside the creature's abdomen. Slimy, cold guts oozed against my skin, sliding through my fingers like snot. It took some doing to work myself to a vertical position so I could reach high enough to get my claws through the tougher armor on its back. Fortunately, digging my way through from the inside was a lot easier than trying to get through the hardened plates from outside. After some frantic clawing and ripping, the plates gave way above me and I thrust my face upward into the cool, clean air. I gasped in a breath, then coughed as the stench of the scorpion's innards hit me. Goddess, that was nasty.

I climbed through the hole I'd made, clambered up onto the creature's back, and hopped down onto the artificial turf. Slime dripped from my body, and I shook my arms to rid myself of some of it. *Disgusting,* I thought.

The beast's tail twitched as nerve impulses stuttered through its shredded nervous system. I gave it plenty of room, just in case one of those twitches got ambitious, but the creature settled and lay still. I watched it for half a minute, but when it stayed dead, I relaxed.

What the hell was this doing here? When a sorcerer calls a demon, they do it for a specific reason: most often, to kill someone. But there are tons of easier ways to do that, and scores of demons that won't call attention to themselves like a bull-sized scorpion would. Sorcerers generally like to keep things on the down-low. It was the middle of the week in an empty stadium—who was its target?

My eyes narrowed as realization hit me, and I cast an illusion out of reflex. To anyone watching, it would have seemed that I'd started towards the hole in the fence to make my escape, but I never moved. I hid myself under a veil of shadows, unseen and unheard, while my illusory copy did the walking. I stayed where I was, motionless and silent, hidden by my magick as I cast out my senses, searching for anything or anyone that might be nearby.

A ripple of cold jittered down my spine as I touched something that shouldn't have been there. *That's not good.* My eyes darted upwards and I found the source of the ill-feeling. A figure stood atop the huge, rectangular scoreboard, wrapped head-to-toe in a dark, full-length cloak. Even better, it held a tall staff in a black-gloved hand. Oily, dark energy swirled around the eldritch weapon, a scarlet and emerald haze visible to my Fae sight.

I took my first step towards it, intending to use my considerable powers of stealth to get a closer look, and possibly use my claws again, and its head snapped towards me. Twin dots of glaring greenish light regarded me from the shadows within the hood, but its face remained unclear. It raised one hand, and the sharp tingle of magick surrounded me. I found myself completely immobile, my limbs frozen in place. A deep rumble of laughter drifted down to greet me.

"Not bad, GrimFaerie," His voice carried a hint of the deep South, cultured and musical. "You had me fooled there for a moment, but I'm no apprentice. I see you."

I gritted my teeth and allowed my anger to build. I didn't like being controlled. In fact, it royally pissed me off. Taking a breath, I focused on the energy that held my body still. It was strong, yes, and it had also taken me by surprise. I assessed it carefully, feeling out the spell. Having been attacked often over the centuries, I've learned a few things. When I had its measure, I flexed my magick within me, focusing its power to attack the spell's structure. It took far more energy than I liked, but the newcomer's spell shattered like crystal, freeing me. The cloaked figure grunted as if struck, making me smile. Then a wave of exhaustion hit, dropping me to one knee and surprising me at how much the effort had taxed me. *Wow, the guy's got skills. And power.*

Not wanting to show weakness, I willed myself to my feet and burst into as fast a run as I could manage. I knew I had little chance of reaching him, but it was worth a shot.

"Impressive," the cloaked one raised his voice in surprise, some of his culture momentarily worn away. He recovered quickly, though. "Yes, you'll definitely be of use to me. You can have this round, Grim. But soon, you'll bow to me in earnest. You'll pledge yourself to me before this is done. I've got work for you to do." He slashed the end of his staff through the air, and a glowing red line appeared. The line widened into a slim rectangle of scarlet light, a doorway to somewhere else. Black Cloak stepped into the light and closed the portal after him, leaving nothing but darkness behind.

Chapter 2

"Wow, it sounds like you had fun last night. So, you have no idea who this guy was?" Ariana said, leaning forward in her chair. She brushed a lock of blonde hair out of her eyes and tucked it behind one ear.

"No," I said, "His face was hidden. Even so, I can recognize a sorcerer by the feel of their magick the same way we can tell someone by their voice, but I've never met this one before. He seems to know me, though. And that's bothersome."

"It is," she agreed, leaning back and propping her bare feet up on the porch railing. "I mean, no one's supposed to know you. You're a Fae assassin, right? Secrecy is kind of your thing. Even those who know of your kind probably wouldn't know you personally."

"Exactly. Very few know of our existence, and even fewer know me by any of my names. Most who've ever met me are dead."

That comment might have bothered anyone else, but Ariana only nodded and took a swig of beer from the bottle she'd brought outside. She was a tough Texas girl, to hear her tell it. I'd known her for a couple of years and felt that was a decent assessment. No matter where she hailed from, she'd proven her worth in my eyes several times over. I'd seen her stab a huge zombie troll to death with a broomstick, which had been both helpful and entertaining. Not only was she capable of taking out oversized thugs with her Krav Maga and jiu jitsu skills, the girl could also shoot like Annie Oakley, who had been a much nicer lady than anyone gave her credit for. Ariana was the last in a long line of witches, and well-trained in magickal arts as well. More importantly, because this kind of thing doesn't come easily to a GrimFaerie, she was my friend. I still wore my human illusion around her, though. No sense in weirding people out.

"Well," she said, shaking her head, "whoever this guy is, it sounds like he has plans for you. I wish we had some idea of what to do next."

I sighed. I hated waiting. I mean, don't get me wrong, sometimes you have to exercise extreme patience as an assassin. I'm fully capable of that. Just because I can do it, doesn't mean I like it. I'm much happier with an immediate target and a plan of action, something I can sink my claws into.

"Yes, so do I," I agreed. "I did what I could to trace him, but he covered his tracks well enough. And I couldn't tell much from the demon before the body disintegrated. The guy was testing me, that much is obvious. He even said as much. He could have been lying, of course, but it felt like he was telling the truth."

Ariana frowned. "So, he knows you're a bad-ass and thinks he can, what? Make you work for him?"

"Make me his servant," I corrected.

"Could he do that?"

I shook my head, not liking that idea at all. "I'd have to agree to it. Contracts are binding in the world of Faerie. He could make me do anything if I agreed to do so. The terms would have to be spelled out pretty clearly, though. Very precisely worded. It's the letter of the law, not the spirit of it, that concerns my kind." The thought of having to do someone else's bidding, to be at their beck and call, repulsed me. "But," I allowed a smile to appear as I continued, "There are ways to be exceedingly difficult within that kind of framework. Depending on how smart he was in giving me commands, I could make him beg to be rid of me. We're good at finding loopholes. But even so, I'd never willingly agree to something like that. The possibilities are"—I frowned—"distasteful." I didn't mention that I could be ordered to kill people. My entire job is killing, but all of my chosen targets deserve it, one hundred percent. I don't kill innocents. Having to kill people that might not deserve it was against the rules. My rules. I make them and only I get to break them if I want. And I don't.

"Yeah, I don't take orders well, either." Ariana sipped at her beer again and wiggled her toes, apparently enjoying the feel of the cool breeze against them. "And the scorpion-thing?"

I shrugged. "Disintegrated a couple minutes after I killed it. A garden variety demon, really."

Ariana shook her head. "I never thought I'd see the day when I heard of a tractor-sized scorpion demon referred to as 'garden variety,' but there it is." She brought her feet down from the railing and stood, taking a moment to stretch her lithe, athletic body in a graceful arc. She moved like a swimmer or a dancer, smooth muscles playing beneath sun-tanned skin. Not quite thirty, she was what most would call 'cute,' but a glint of danger surfaced in her eyes now and then—a glint I recognized well. Ariana might look like an ordinary, fit young woman, but her combat skills gained much more of my respect than her sinuous curves. "Hey, you're staring. Not nice." She smiled when she said it.

"Apologies," I said without shame, "I wasn't being creepy. Just admiring, my friend. You've been training harder, haven't you? Put on some muscle?"

Ariana shrugged a shoulder that I knew for a fact hadn't been so well-defined when we'd first met. She flashed a smile at me, pleased I'd noticed. "You can tell? Really?"

"Indeed," I replied. "You've become close friends with those cannonball things. Kettlebells, right?"

"Yep!" she confirmed. "They really do the trick, too. I'm strong as a very feminine, sexy ox!" She flexed in an imitation of a bodybuilder. "Grrrr! See?"

Before I could answer, she loudly smacked her own bottom, laughed at herself, then went inside for another beer, leaving me alone with my thoughts on the porch.

She'd been seeing Maximus Von Gerhardt of late. He was a werewolf. Wait, that's not really correct. . .he was THE werewolf. The king of them all, as it were. To my knowledge, he was the oldest and the strongest of them, and that meant he was a force of nature set well apart from humanity. I've only tangled with a few, and although I'd killed each one, none of them went down easily. It had been close each time, and although each had been a formidable beast, they'd also been young and unskilled.

Max was neither.

Not only was Von Gerhardt an enormous and powerful specimen, he had been around for centuries. He'd had time to explore his animal nature inside and out. He knew himself and he knew the full capabilities of his gift. He could fight impressively well both as a man and a beast. In addition, he was also acquainted with certain types of magick, at the very least well enough to protect himself. Folks who got on his bad side regretted it if they lived long enough.

Fortunately, along with being powerful, wealthy, and well-connected, Max was also a truly noble soul, one of the few I'd encountered having such wealth and status. A kind and benevolent ruler, he guided his businesses and his werewolf clan with such wisdom and compassion that it bred fierce loyalty among his people. All in all, he was a pretty cool guy. For a werewolf.

And he'd managed to become Ariana's boyfriend, a fact which seemed to please them both mightily. I knew they hadn't quite gone there yet, which completely baffled me, but then humans baffled me more often than not. Ariana once told me that her previous relationship had been complicated, so maybe that had something to do with it. I sighed, wondering when Ariana would pull her

13

head out of her ass and just jump the guy. Maybe warn him first so he didn't bite her.

I smiled at that and brought my thoughts back to the situation at hand. There was a sorcerer out there with sufficient skill to throw an enormous demon at me before using a dimensional portal to make his exit. I rolled the night's events over in my mind. *What does it mean?*

The sound of a car engine caught my attention and pulled me out of my musing. The noise filtered in from far away, but steadily approached. Ariana's homestead sat in the middle of a large and heavily forested spread of land left untouched since the 1800s. Her witchy family had chosen a site far enough outside of what would eventually be Houston that no one would bother them. If I could hear the car, there was no mistake—it followed the one and only road that led to Ariana's farmhouse.

I rose from my chair and dimmed myself. It's a simple veil, a spell that renders me hard to see unless you knew exactly where to look but takes far less effort than a true invisibility spell. Ariana hadn't told me she was expecting company, and I don't like surprises. Too many of them have sharp teeth. I moved down the steps and ambled toward the little car Ariana tended to zip around town in: a Mini Cooper, she called it. I walked over and stood behind it, not bothering to crouch down. The car and my veil were cover enough. I'd be able to see the newcomer in plenty of time find out who they were and detain them if need be. Or kill them if it came to that. I slipped my claws out and flexed them once, but pulled them back into my fingertips. *No need to be impolite,* I thought as I stared at the opening in the trees where I knew the car would emerge.

A sleek black SUV that I didn't recognize rolled into view moments later. It looked new, and the tinted windows kept me from seeing the driver. I waited. It pulled up behind the Cooper and I heard the engine shut down. My knees flexed out of habit as I prepared to spring, and the door opened.

A woman emerged from the car. Not tall, she looked only about 5 foot 4, and sturdily built. Upon first glance, one might have thought her curves were built on the couch, but she moved with the smooth grace of an athlete and the assurance of one who knew their way around a fight. The fading sunlight struck hair so black it shined almost blue. Stylishly cut short in the back, leaving the front long on both sides, her raven hair framed a stern, but pretty face. Eyes the color of the sea in the Mediterranean, a pale greenish-blue that could fade almost to gray in bright light or deepen into pale emerald if she were upset, glittered with intelligence. A polo shirt of deep green tidily tucked into men's black pants complimented her eyes, though they didn't need the help. A detective badge glinted on her belt, and I noted the gun on her right hip. She opened the rear hatch of the car, pulled a small duffel from it, and slipped the strap over her shoulder as she slammed the door shut. She took a few steps toward the porch, then stopped as though she'd heard something.

Her right hand eased up to rest on the butt of her gun as she scanned the house. She stayed that way for a few moments, watching and listening. Those pale eyes found their way towards me and my heartbeat quickened as she turned in my direction. I saw her squint in confusion as she tried to figure out what had attracted her attention. I used the opportunity to observe her. She stood ready and watchful, and I found myself admiring her. Although strong, her femininity enchanted me, and the faintest touch of eyeliner highlighted her beauty more than it should have. I followed the lines and curves of her face, enjoying the sight of her before I grimaced at my indulgence. I squeezed my eyes shut and I got a tighter grip on myself. Humans are beneath my notice. Or they should be.

Dammit, I thought. *Why does she do that to me?*

She continued staring in my direction as she tried to focus, puzzlement plain on her face. "Kane? Is that you?"

Impressive, I thought, *she can't see me, but still senses that I'm here. Training with Ariana has taught her much.*

I dropped the veil and relished her slight gasp of startlement. "Hello, Avery. Nice to see you again."

She recovered and smiled. I noticed a butterfly flitting around in my stomach. Maybe more than one.

Her smile is doing things to me that it shouldn't. Why? I shook off the feeling. It must have shown on my face (my illusory one, anyway) because Avery raised an eyebrow.

"Nice to see you too. You, um. . .you ok?"

I shook it off and focused on the task at hand. "I am, considering I was attacked by a scorpion demon last night. And there's a sorcerer out there who wants to make me his personal lackey." I expected Avery to be surprised, but she nodded instead.

"I thought that was you. Yes, I heard there was some kind of disturbance at Legacy Stadium. Nobody saw anything when it happened, but the fence around the field was ripped open like a baby Godzilla had been through it. There were strange marks in the parking lot and on the field, scuffs and gashes that looked too big for anything smaller than construction equipment to make, and some weird burns as well." She smiled, her eyes catching the afternoon light and sparkling. "Scorpion demon, I suppose?"

"Indeed," I replied. I realized she was alone. "Say, where's Jim? Shouldn't he be with you?"

Avery laughed, "Bastard's on vacation. Up and hopped a plane with the wife and kids and hauled ass to Florida to play in the blue water."

I nodded. I'd only known Jim Kaley as long as I'd known Avery, and he'd proven to be a solid cop, if a little soft around the middle. His heart was in the right place, though. And he had guts. He'd proven that in New Mexico when he'd wanted to go back after Avery even though he'd been thoroughly beaten, dehydrated, exhausted, and had a demon exorcised from his body. If he wanted a vacation, he probably deserved it. To Avery, I said, "So have you been assigned to the case?"

She shook her head, making the tips of her hair sway on either side of her face. "No, the surveillance footage went wonky around the time they thought it happened, so they pretty much chalked it up to wayward youth. They increased patrols in that area for the next couple of weeks, but they don't expect to catch anyone for it." She folded her arms, leaned against the hood of Ariana's car, and folded one ankle over the other, a picture of relaxation. "But I could feel the magick in the air. It was faint, but it had a nasty taint to it." She continued in a softer voice, "Wanna tell me about it?"

I relayed the events of the previous evening as succinctly as I could. Before she could answer, a cheery voice called from the house, "Detective Lynne, it's great to see you!" Ariana came back out on the porch, holding a fresh beer in one hand and a glass of water for me in the other. "Come on inside, I'll get you something. Have you been doing your exercises?"

Avery smiled and dramatically rolled her eyes before winking at me. "Yes, teacher, I've been a good girl. Every morning and night. And call me Avery, I'm off duty"

Avery wasn't a witch. She was—well, I still wasn't sure what she was, to be honest. In terms of brute magickal muscle, she was far stronger than Ariana, who'd spent her life training in spellcraft. For all her strength, she was unschooled. She couldn't access her power consistently and was ignorant of the more scholarly ways of using magick. Her intuition was off the charts, bordering on precognition at times, and she had other talents that led me to believe there had to be some Fae in her bloodline. If that was true, the exact circumstances of that influence were a mystery to all of us, Avery included. We knew her grandfather had been a practitioner of the magickal arts, but as far as we knew he'd been human. Sadly, he'd proven to be a *bad* human prone to using his skills and powers to harm others. I know this because I'd been sent to kill him. I'd done my job with my usual thoroughness, but I'd been seen by a much younger Avery. She'd been a little girl at the time. Witnessed the whole thing.

I'd made a big impression because she'd instantly recognized me the next time we'd crossed paths. She remembered both versions of me, the human illusion I habitually wore, and *me*, my true self. I'd been in her nightmares for years, and although I hadn't known her when we'd met up again, she'd recognized the monster in me right away. I mean, I'd killed her grandfather right in front of her when she was a young girl, and in grand, messy fashion. That made it difficult for her to trust me at first, as you might expect.

However, after all that happened in New Mexico last year, she seemed to abandon any ill will from her grandfather's death. After much discussion, some things came to light that made sense. He'd probably been about to sacrifice her to some demon at the time, which is one of the few reasons a Grim would be sent to deal with him. Although I didn't remember the specifics, I don't make mistakes where my targets are concerned, so I knew he'd earned his punishment. And it seemed Avery believed that too.

"Ariana says you've been progressing well," I said as we made our way to the porch. "What's she got you working on now?"

Avery laughed ruefully, "Creating magickal tools. She's really amazing at enchanting things. She told me about that snow globe she used when you guys went after Elias Bress. I. . ." she paused as if to find the right words, "I want to make a wand. You know, to help me channel my power."

"A magick wand? Won't that look a little odd sticking out of your belt next to your gun?" I teased. Wands had been around for thousands of years, but in today's world, they were more than a little out of place.

Avery blushed. "Hey, it's just a thought. I'm not sure how I blasted that bitch back in the cave, but Ariana's got some ideas. She thinks a wand might help me focus so I can use that power more precisely. I don't want to have anything happen by accident."

I nodded as I pulled the door open for her. She'd thrown as big a blast of pure force as I'd seen any witch or sorcerer throw in decades, and she'd done it out of pure anger and frustration without any idea of what she was doing. "That sounds like a good plan," I agreed. *Anything that'll keep you safe,* I added silently. As I realized what I'd thought, I nearly stopped walking, surprised at myself. *Where'd that come from?*

Ariana shoved a water glass at me, and I accepted it as she handed an opened beer to Avery. She beamed at us both, oblivious to my discomfort. "So, what's up, lady? You know I'm happy to see you, but you could have just texted."

Avery sipped at the bottle gratefully, then set it down on a coaster on the table. Her gaze flicked back at me as she replied, "Kane just told me about last night. I was telling him that I'd been out to the stadium where he had his run-in with that, um, scorpion demon, was it?" I

19

nodded and she continued. "I found something that I wanted to show both of you, so I'm glad you were here together. Here, take a look." She set the duffle on the table, unzipped it, then pulled an evidence bag from within. She gently laid it on the table so we could get a look at the pale, circular object inside.

"I'm almost positive that's bone," Avery murmured as she pulled on a pair of nitrile gloves. "I wanted you guys to see it first because it feels bad. Wrong, somehow. I didn't let the others know I found it."

I'd felt the faint, but distinct tingle of foul magick the moment it had come into view. Whatever the piece was, it had most certainly been used in some sort of ritual or spell casting. I stayed silent as I watched her open the bag and extract a disc of bone a little smaller than the palm of my hand. A slight concavity made the piece into a shallow, somewhat irregular bowl. Avery held it up between two fingers and showed us the markings on its underside.

Ariana spoke first. "Oh, yeah, those are definitely bad news runes. You found it in the parking lot?"

Avery nodded. "Yes, on the east side."

"That's where it appeared and attacked me," I confirmed.

"What brought you out to the area?" Avery inquired. "You're staying on the other side of the freeway, right?"

"Tacos," I answered. They both stared at me as if I'd said something strange and I frowned. "What? There's a little Mexican market on Franz that has great tacos. I wanted some. I was passing through the stadium parking lot on my way there when the demon appeared."

"They don't have tacos on your side of town?" Ariana teased.

"Not like Picacho's," I said simply.

I find most human food to be bland, but Picacho's tacos were delicious. I'd been there so often lately that when I'd skipped a few days in a row, one of the ladies stomped her foot when I reappeared and said, "Where were you, we were worried!" I smiled at the memory.

Avery smiled but shook her head. "That's interesting. If you've been going there often, someone noticed the pattern. More importantly, they knew what you are. Any ideas who that might have been?" She placed the plastic bag on the table and laid the bone artifact on it.

I shook my head. "No, I didn't recognize him. He had a Southern accent, but I didn't spend much time in places where that was prevalent."

Ariana laughed, "Well, you didn't have to spend much time anywhere to piss someone off. You're good at that. Very efficient."

I couldn't argue that. Where I went, people died. Granted, they were all bad people, but even bad people often had someone who cared about them. Maybe someone held a grudge. "True," I agreed. "Even so, I generally hide my tracks well and don't leave loose ends."

"Unless there are tacos involved," Avery nudged me with an elbow and grinned.

I gave her some serious side-eye but kept from commenting. Instead, I reached one hand towards the bone fragment.

Avery reached out and touched my arm, stopping me. She raised an eyebrow. "Gloves?" she asked.

"Not necessary. I don't leave prints."

Avery shrugged and removed her hand from my arm, and I returned my attention to the piece of bone on the table. Unprotected by the plastic, it reeked of foul magick, giving off the same psychic impression as the power I'd felt emanating from the cowled figure in the stadium. I reached for it again, intending to pick it up and examine it more closely. Just before I touched it, I heard Avery gasp. "Wait!"

Too late.

A brilliant green and yellow light exploded from the bone, blinding and ferocious. Avery and Ariana flinched away, covering their faces with their arms, but I was frozen, arrested by the power I set free. The green-gold energy swirled over my fingers, inching its way up my hand, then my arm. I tried to pull away, but it was too strong. It held me immobile, helpless.

An intense, burning cold crawled over my body, accelerating as it swarmed over every inch of my skin. The unknown energy explored me, penetrated my body as it flowed through every cell, every fiber. I clenched my jaws shut as agony rippled through me. I couldn't breathe, I couldn't think, only endure the pain.

The energy shifted, moved, flowed towards my wrists where it concentrated in blinding bands of light, forcing me to squeeze my eyes shut against the searing glare. The intense hum of power rose into an incredible crescendo, a roar that beat at my eardrums and forced Ariana and Avery to cover their ears with their hands. I screamed, a wordless cry of pain and anguish that was shut out by the growing noise of the magick that gripped me. When I thought I'd reached my limit, the flare of magick vanished. Darkness flooded the room as a deafening silence fell. My stomach clenched itself into a vicious knot and I bent over, gagging, my senses completely overwhelmed. The impact of my body hitting the floor was a distant sensation, another noise for my overloaded brain to sort out later. *Much later.* I blacked out.

"Kane!" Avery's panicked voice cut through the haze in my mind and I struggled towards it. I'd never heard her like that. Scared. Almost terrified. "Kane, what happened? Are you. . .oh my god. . .are you hurt? Can. . .can you hear me? Help me! Help him!"

I felt her hands on me, touching my neck, my arms, my chest. I tried to sit up and found that I had to let her help me more than I liked. The depth of my weakness horrified me.

"I'm OK," I growled, then frowned at the sound of my own voice. It didn't sound right. Or rather, it sounded far too much like my actual voice. My undisguised voice. My vision was still blurry, and I blinked a few times as I tried to get my eyes to focus.

Ariana appeared on my other side and got her hands around my free arm. The two women heaved me to my feet, and I stumbled towards the table. I put my hands on the thick wooden surface and leaned heavily on it, exhausted.

Avery spoke, her voice quiet and astonished. "Kane, you're. . .wow. So that's what you really look like. I've seen you like that before, but never. . .like this, close up."

I glanced at her, confused, then I glanced back at my hands on the table. It took a moment for me to realize what I was seeing, and when I did, my stomach dropped beyond my feet. My glamour had been broken.

I stared at my real hands. My skin was blue-black, the fingers long and grasping. My bone claws were still hidden within my fingertips, but a simple flex would extend the razor-sharp talons. They were powerfully made. *For killing,* I absently thought. The sight of my undisguised hands confused me, terrified me, infuriated me. *This isn't right.*

Above my hands, two new cuffs, wide bands of carved bone, encircled each wrist. Eldritch runes had been inscribed into the pale white surface of each, and they felt far heavier than they looked. I picked up one hand and turned it over. The cuff had no seam, no clasp, just a solid chunk of bone somehow fashioned into a tight band about four inches long. The kind of band a prisoner might wear.

I looked up and saw Avery looking at my hands as well. Her eyes lifted to mine, and I quickly averted my gaze. Without a word, I turned and left the kitchen, heading for the relative privacy of the living room.

My feelings were an unaccustomed jumble, and for reasons I didn't yet understand, I didn't want her to see me like this. I couldn't meet her eyes, not yet.

I didn't want to see the fear in them.

Chapter 3

"Thank you for the garments," I mumbled, pulling the hood of the sweatshirt as far over my head as I could. I needed the shadows it provided, and I'd already wrapped the thin scarf around my face. The black cotton gloves Ariana found for me looked odd on my overlong fingers, and I couldn't feel anything through them, which further aggravated me. I caught a glimpse of myself in the dresser mirror and realized that I looked like I was about to rob a bank.

"Hey, no worries," Ariana replied. She put a hand on my arm but removed it when I reflexively stiffened. She was silent a few moments, then kept her voice low, "Look, it's fine. You don't need to wear this stuff here. I don't care what you look like. You're my friend."

I didn't reply. I'd taken care to hide my true self from her ever since we met. I reminded myself that, as she said, she was my friend. If any human would accept my true appearance, I figured she would. Even so, I still felt the need to cover myself.

What deeply troubled me was that whatever the bone wristbands were, they completely suppressed my ability to cast illusions. That was like taking away my ability to read. I wasn't right without it. I wasn't me. In addition, I had no idea what other effects the cuffs might have, but I already felt crippled. It weighed heavily.

I carefully avoided thinking about Avery. I didn't want her to see me this way. The fact that it was even an issue with me warranted some intense internal discussion, but that was for another day. At least she hadn't run screaming, as many had in the past.

"Thanks," I managed. "Any ideas?"

"You might want some sunglasses if you go out in public," she chirped, offering a sly smile, "Those shiny eyes are wicked cool, but you probably don't want anyone outside this house to see them." She turned to her dresser, snagged a pair of dark glasses, and handed them to me. "Here. You owe me twenty bucks if you break 'em."

I sighed and allowed the tiniest hint of amusement to appear within the deep well of foreboding I'd cultivated. I turned my quicksilver eyes her way and when she didn't look away, I smiled behind the scarf, glad that she couldn't see my fangs. "I accept your bargain, human. Use of your glasses against the offer of payment in the event they come to harm. I thank thee." I bowed at the waist.

Ariana rolled her eyes and tossed her blonde ponytail in mock exasperation. "Stuff it, Shakespeare." She cocked her head to one side as she looked me over. "It's good to really see you like this for more than a few seconds. Your true self, I mean. I'd caught glimpses now and then. I always knew you had a glamour on, but until now, you always managed to keep me from seeing you." Then she winked at me and added, "Well, you *thought* you did. Let's go figure this thing out."

She flounced out of the bedroom leaving me standing there, dumbfounded. I'd thought I'd done a decent job of hiding my true form from her. I'd been veiling myself around humans for centuries, and I was damned good at it. I sighed, then amended, *Most of the time, anyway.* She'd apparently seen me at some point, and it didn't seem to faze her at all. A weird little spark burst into life somewhere in my heart. *Maybe Avery would feel the same.* I made a face and shook my head as I sternly reminded myself that I didn't give a shit what Avery thought. Why would I? I growled, then followed Ariana out of the bedroom and down the stairs, sliding the glasses into place as I went.

I entered the kitchen a few steps behind Ariana. The moment I appeared, Avery bolted up from her chair, concern written all over her face.

"Kane!" I heard the relief in her voice, and my stupid heart did a little flip. "Kane, you're all right!" She held her hands clasped together, worrying at the thumbnail on her left hand. It looked pretty ragged. She took a step towards me, and I stopped abruptly. She stopped as well, uncertain and breathless.

"I'm fine." I assured her, trying to keep the growl out of my voice. "Aside from losing my magick." I held out my wrists. "I've got to get these things off me. And then I'm going to find that sorcerer and. . ." My voice trailed off as my emotions got the better of me. *Oh, I'll make him pay, all right. Dearly.*

Avery's voice shifted into a more businesslike tone as the detective in her emerged. "So, what are those, exactly? Do you know how they work?"

I sighed and held them out so she could see them better. She stepped closer and took my gloved hands in hers so she could examine the cuffs. I found myself wishing I could feel her skin, but the gloves were in the way.

As best I could, I told her what I knew. "That was an impressively wrought trap to have been set to spring at my touch only. At least the cuffs aren't connected with a chain. That would have made this even worse." I paused, thinking. "I've never seen manacles like this before. They're solid all the way around, so there's no lock to pick. They've been enspelled. I can feel a faint vibration from them, an energy. As much as I'd like to try smashing these with a hammer, I have a sneaking suspicion that wouldn't end well. And as you can see, they—they nullify my ability to cast glamours."

"Bastard," Avery said, letting some real heat seep into the curse. "We'll find him and rip his balls off."

27

"I'm totally on board with that plan," Ariana muttered from where she leaned against one wall. "Let's make sure he removes those cuffs first, though."

Avery glanced over my shoulder at Ariana and I got a good look at her eyes. They'd deepened into an intense sea green. "Is there anything you can do? You're great with enchanted objects, surely there's something?"

"Maybe," Ariana replied, "I'll need to get Kane into my conjuring room, and we'll see what's what. Of course, I'll need to be awfully careful since we just don't know what we're dealing with."

Before I could reply, something caught my attention. The bone cuffs might have messed up my glamours, but there was nothing wrong with my hearing. "There's a car coming," I said as I turned to Ariana. "Are you expecting someone?"

Ariana's face fell into a serious mask. Moving with impressive grace and efficiency, she opened a nearby drawer and removed a burly-looking handgun in a paddle holster. "No, I am not." She checked the magazine and racked a round into the chamber before carefully tucking the holster into the small of her back and making sure the weapon was securely seated.

As Avery made sure her own firearm was accessible and ready, the sounds I heard from faraway became audible inside the house. It sounded like a small car, moving without haste. We all moved to the front window and saw a little brown vehicle pull into her driveway, its headlights visible in the deep shadows of the surrounding trees. I counted two figures inside: a driver and a passenger in the back seat.

I turned to Ariana, "Can you throw a veil over me?"

Ariana made a face. "Sure, but a quick one won't be fancy at all. I'm not nearly as good at those as you are."

"As I was, you mean," I corrected her. "Do it."

Avery moved to the door and pushed the curtain aside so she could see better. "It looks like an Uber. I can see the sticker in the window." She added, "Guy getting out of the back. Caucasian, tall. Looks more than a little scruffy. He's got dark glasses on and, and. . .he's got a white cane." She turned back to us, perplexed. "I think he might be blind." Returning her gaze to the yard, she watched for a few moments then continued, "He's just standing by the car. He's got something in his hand, I can't quite see what."

Ariana listened but kept her eyes on me, her face a mask of concentration as she prepared to cast a veiling spell. A gesture and a few archaic syllables later, her power washed over me in a tingling rush. I looked down at my arms and found that I was nearly invisible. If I kept behind either of them, I wouldn't be seen at all. I looked up at Ariana and found her with arms folded and a self-satisfied look on her face.

"There ya go! It ain't perfect, but no one'll see you out there."

Avery chuckled. "I doubt it'll matter to our visitor, but it pays to avoid taking chances. The driver, at least, would certainly notice that outfit. Y'all ready?" She opened the door, leaving it open so I could slip out between her and Ariana as we exited the house.

The car was still idling, the driver concealed behind a tinted window. As Avery had said, the passenger was standing next to the vehicle with the door open. He seemed a bit taller than average height and sported a messy fringe of dirty blond hair that ringed a bald pate. His deeply lined face had been burned into leather by the sun, and his stubbly beard looked as unkempt as the rest of him. The man had a weary and worn look about him, and the smell was. . .bad.

Homeless, I thought, *and not an ounce of magick in him. This isn't our guy.*

29

The man wore sunglasses, and he held a dirty but distinctive cane, white with red at the bottom end. The hand that held it shook visibly. The other held a large manila envelope.

Hearing our approach, he turned his face towards us and spoke in a gravelly voice. "Uh, hello? I'm supposed to find someone named Kane?"

We marched across the yard until we were a few yards away from the man and stopped. Ariana spoke up. "He's not here. Can I help you?"

The man turned as she spoke and held out the envelope. "Uh, are you, um, Ariana?"

"Who wants to know?"

"I'm Carl," he began, "Carl Jenkins. A guy said he'd pay me two hundred bucks to take this Uber here and hand this to either Kane or Ariana."

Avery interrupted, "What guy? His name?"

Carl shook his head, "No, ma'am. He didn't say. But it was easy money, so here I am."

"Where was this?" Avery's detective voice was harder, lower. It gave me feels until I made them stop.

"Oh, it was, um. . ." Carl's voice trailed off and his brow wrinkled. "I was. . .that's weird. I can't remember."

Avery strode over to the driver's window and rapped sharply on the dark glass, resting one hand rather obviously on her gun. The window whirred as it lowered, revealing a young, meek-looking little man with curly blond hair and glasses. Avery flashed her badge, and his eyes went wide. "License and registration," she asked, and the driver fumbled out his wallet. She snatched the license from his fingers and examined it. She took a picture of it with her phone before handing it back. "Where'd you find him?" She took a few pictures of Carl while she waited for the driver to answer.

"At Walgreens, corner of Franz and Katyland in old Katy," he stammered, "Here, look." He presented his phone and showed Avery the screen. She looked at it for a moment, then back at the young man.

"Anyone else around?"

"No ma'am! He was waiting outside the Walgreens, just like you see him."

She sighed and shook her head. Turning to Ariana, she said, "Nothing there. The app just shows his name, Carl. Nothing else."

Carl spoke up again, "Can I give this to Ariana or Kane so I can go?"

"Here, let me have it," Ariana said, moving forward to take the envelope from his shaking hand, "but stick around for a couple minutes, we still have questions." She hesitated as she reached for it, and I felt her assessing it, searching it for magickal traps. I'd been fooled once, and she didn't want to make a similar mistake. After a few tense seconds, she accepted it. He sighed with relief and let his hand drop to his side.

Ariana looked around for me, but the veil was doing its job. Her voice echoed in my mind a moment later.

There's magick here, but it's far less than the bone thing from earlier. I doubt it's a threat. This just feels like paper.

Avery chimed in. Apparently, Ariana had taught her our trick of speaking mind-to-mind. And she was *loud*.

I should run him in. See who he is. He might know something that could help us.

I shook my head, then remembered she couldn't see me. *No, I need you here,* I paused as I saw a surprised expression appear on her face, and I amended, *We. We need you here. I can search his mind to see if he knows anything.*

You can do that? Avery asked, her surprise coming through.

Well, yes, I can. Most of the time. There are a few extraordinarily strong-minded humans that can keep me out, and those with the proper training such as Ariana, definitely could. But I had a hunch that Carl wasn't going to be much of a problem for me to read. Or a help, either.

I looked back at Carl. *Yes, give me a second and I'll see if I can dig any info out of his mind. It won't hurt him or anything, I'm just checking to see what he remembers.*

Reaching out with my magick, I entered Carl's mind and found a simple fellow with an overwhelming desire to do nothing more than go to McDonald's and wolf down a burger. He was nervous as hell, but only because this was all out of the ordinary for him, and as a blind man, he found safety and security in his routine. I sifted through his memories to see what I could find, which was limited to Carl's senses of touch, hearing, and smell. I'd never gone into a blind person's mind before, and it was unnerving. His remaining senses were hyperaware, and it took a moment for me to adjust to his memories without a visual reference point. I growled in frustration but kept digging, hoping I'd get something useful. The Uber ride was most recent, so that was easy to place, then I felt the pavement beneath his feet, presumably at the Walgreens. I was only able to put it together because of the driver's information and because I'd just been out there the night before. The place was only a stone's throw from the parking lot where I'd battled the scorpion demon.

Beyond that, nothing. A blank. I kept sifting and found a memory from hours earlier, our buddy Carl walking on a concrete surface next to running water, by the sound of it. I listened intently, borrowing Carl's enhanced hearing, and guessed he had been near one of the branches of Mason Creek. There were a couple of bridges that didn't have jogging paths, and small homeless contingents had staked their claims at each one.

Carl's thoughts told me that it had been this morning, but after that, there was nothing until he found himself waiting for the Uber at Walgreens. Carl truly had no idea who gave him the money. It had been wiped as clean as a new whiteboard in there, aside from the pertinent information of the job at hand. As far as I could tell, he was harmless.

Nothing, I sent to both Ariana and Avery, *he doesn't remember any of it. He's nobody. You can let him walk. We need to see what's in the envelope, but not out here. Open it in the house where it's safe.*

Ariana caught Avery's eye and they shared a look, then Ariana turned back to Carl. "Is there anything else you're supposed to tell us?"

He shook his head. "No, ma'am. Just come here and give you that, 'sall I was told to do."

Avery dismissed him, "All right then. You can take off."

Carl bobbed his head in thanks then got back into the car and shut the door. After some bickering between Carl and the driver, Carl pulled some money out of a dirty pocket and settled the matter. The car backed up and turned its nose outward, heading out the same way it had come, leaving all of us staring at a large manila envelope.

~

Ariana used a pair of kitchen tongs to pull a single sheet of thick paper from the envelope and laid it in the small conjuring circle she had built into a table for up-close work. Murmuring quietly, she sent a bit of her will into the circle and it came to life, a half-dome of energy that kept magick of any kind from crossing its boundary. I'd sensed the power embedded in the paper when she'd brought it out and noted that it lacked the darker, more intense feeling the bone artifact had given off. There were

33

enough hints of the same magick, however, that I recognized its connection to the manacles I wore. They'd all most certainly been created by the same person. I leaned closer and examined the elegant script that covered the parchment in graceful whorls and lines. Standing at my shoulder, Avery did the same.

"Very artistic, this guy," Avery said, sarcasm dripping from the words.

I removed Ariana's sunglasses and set them aside. *The hell with it,* I thought. *They're my friends. It's fine.* I leaned closer and read aloud.

"My Dearest Kane,

I'll get right to the point. The cuffs you now wear are my creation, unique in their function. I'm quite proud of them. I had you in mind when I made them, you see, and I think you'll find they fit you perfectly. I've watched you for weeks, and I knew that it was only a matter of time until you came into contact with the 'clue' I left at the scene of our last meeting. I felt it engage and am tickled to inform you that the clock is now running. At midnight tomorrow, the bone manacles around your wrists will do two things: they will snap shut, removing both your hands at the wrists, and they will also permanently nullify your ability to cast illusions. As their creator, only I can remove them without incurring damage. Anyone else who tries will suffer rather severe consequences. I admit, I chuckled as I wrote that. I do hope one of you attempts to remove them. It would amuse me greatly.

Why the manacles, you ask? Well, I have a deal for you. If you accept and complete the task I have in mind, the manacles will open and you will be free. You may keep your hands and your illusory ability and go about your way, never to hear from me again. If not, you'll be lessened by the experience.

Before the deadline, Maximus Lucanis von Gerhardt must die. The method of execution does not matter, only the result. I'm sure you'll find a way.

Prick your thumb and apply a thumbprint in your own blood to this document to seal the bargain. Your ability to cast glamours will be temporarily restored the moment your blood hits the paper. You'll need all of your skills for this mission, so I loan that ability back to you. You now know that you have it at my whim. Use it well. Oh, and I've included a minor attitude enhancer with the cuffs. It should help you stay focused during this little endeavor.

Respectfully yours,

Malleus

PS If you don't agree within thirty minutes of reading this letter, I will take that as an act of noncompliance and the cuffs will do their job sooner rather than later. Make your decision quickly.

"Malleus?" Avery repeated.

"It means hammer in Latin," Ariana rolled her eyes. "His real name is probably something a bit less macho." She turned to me. "Ring any bells?"

I shook my head, "No, none. I'm fairly certain I've never met that guy before. I've no idea how he identified me." I looked at the bone cuffs on my wrists and imagined them cutting off my hands. Not a very pleasant idea.

Concern filled Avery's voice, "Do you think he's telling the truth? Will those things cut off your hands if you don't agree?"

I sighed and looked at Ariana's face, pale with concern. I knew she was going to be conflicted, to say the least. She considered me a friend, as far as I knew, but her relationship with Max had been heating up for a while now. Although his bargain was focused on me, the fact that Malleus had Carl mention the both of us meant that he knew exactly who she was, and likely, her growing affection for Max. Malleus was asking her to choose between the two of us.

Before I could say anything, she frowned with anger and hissed at me, "Do it."

"Are you serious?"

"Yes. Look, we can't take a chance on this. If you sign that paper, it gives us until tomorrow night to find this guy and make him fix it. I know you're not going to hurt Max."

I grimaced. "Even if I were going to, I doubt he'd make it easy for me." I remembered the last time I'd tussled with a werewolf. They're tough. Max would be far more of a challenge, given his age and experience.

Ariana shook her head in frustration, "That's not the point! Look, we need that time to run that asshole down. All we need is the chance. Signing that will give you your powers back and give us the opportunity we need to get you out of this. Otherwise. . ." her voice trailed away as she glanced pointedly down at my hands then back up at me.

I glared at her. "If I sign that, there's no getting out of the deal. You know that. I'm Fae. I either kill Max or lose my hands. There's no getting out of it unless Malleus voluntarily releases me."

She returned my silvery stare with her own of bright blue. "Oh, let me get my hands on him. He'll let you out of it or else wish he had." Whoever he was, Malleus had just made a formidable enemy in Ariana. Underestimating her was usually a mistake.

I looked at Avery and she promptly nodded at me, "I've got vacation time. I'm in. He's not getting away with this, no way in hell." A look flitted across her face, too brief for me to fully interpret.

I paused a moment, thinking, and looked at each woman in turn. Quiet rage boiled within me, forcing me to clench and unclench my hands to stay steady. I'd literally ripped people to pieces for less than what Malleus had already done to me, much less what he was trying to get me to do. But beneath that layer of white-hot anger, my heart gave a little flip at the thought of these two humans that thought so much of me. As much as I hated it, I knew what I had to do. I removed the gloves Ariana loaned me and tossed them aside. I felt Avery's gaze on my hands, long fingered and strong, and not quite human. She looked on, fascinated rather than afraid.

Using my own claw, I pricked my right thumb so that a thick drop of scarlet arose on its surface. I nodded at Ariana, who reached out to break the circle she'd created, removing the protective shield of energy from around the document. I reluctantly picked up the parchment and laid it on the table before me, holding it down with my left hand. I couldn't keep from growling in frustration as I pressed my bleeding thumb to the parchment.

When I pulled my thumb away, I left a perfect crimson thumbprint behind. The paper flared with bright light, forcing me to squint, and when my vision cleared, the contract had vanished. Poof. The atmosphere in the room felt lighter, freer, as if something oppressive had left it. I flexed my will and clothed myself in a glamour, my usual disguise. I watched the skin of my arms and hands take on a human flesh tone as the illusion took shape around me, hiding my darker skin and alien features once more. The cuffs remained visible, their pale ivory surface somehow mocking me with their presence.

I looked at Ariana. "I need you to call Max. He's mixed up in this. He needs to know. And he might have some answers."

Ariana swallowed, then declared, "Right. And if anyone can help us, he can."

I hoped she was right. I really did. Otherwise, I'd have to kill him.

Chapter 4

It took one phone call from Ariana to get Max into one of his helicopters and hurrying south from Dallas. Once he arrived, he quickly set up shop in a hotel near the Galleria area. As the head of a billion-dollar multinational corporation, Max tended to travel in style. The hotel was posh, all glass and steel and marble, and one of the most expensive in town.

After taking the elevator to the top floor, we were met by Edge, Max's pilot and right-hand man. We knew Edge well, having worked with him a few times since we'd rescued Max from Elias Bress's stronghold. He tipped his battered cowboy hat at us and drawled his greetings, which we happily returned, then he ushered us into the penthouse suite.

We found Maximus seated at a cherrywood desk inside, looking dapper as always. An enormous man, muscular and fit, Max wore expensive clothes that didn't have to work hard to flatter him. Silver streaked his black hair at the temples, and a smartly trimmed black beard parted to reveal a handsome smile as we entered. Every movement revealed an animal strength and grace. He stood when we entered, his imposing presence softened by the welcoming smile and delighted laugh that greeted us.

"My friends, it warms my heart to see you!" He came out from around his desk and walked towards us, making a direct line for Ariana. She didn't run into his arms exactly, but I saw a bit of extra hustle in her step, and she let him wrap her in an enveloping hug. They practically had little hearts floating around their heads. I tried not to roll my eyes, but I'm pretty sure I did.

Avery cleared her throat quite obviously, and the pair separated, gazing into each other's eyes for a moment, then regaining their composure. Max turned to Avery and detached himself from Ariana so he could approach her. She extended a hand for him to shake, "Detective Avery Lynne," she declared.

"Thoroughly enchanted, Detective," Max murmured as he gently grasped her fingers and turned her hand over so he could kiss it, "It's a pleasure to meet you at last. Ariana speaks highly of you, and quite often."

Avery's normally stern face lit up in a surprised smile. A rosy glow appeared on her cheeks and I heard her heartbeat accelerate. It took a moment for me to realize she was blushing.

I nearly launched myself at him then and there. Oblivious to my unexpected and instantaneous rage, Avery laughed and made small talk while my heart hammered murderously against my ribs and cold fury raced through my veins like ice water. My claws came out, apparently without conscious thought on my part, though my glamour hid the fact. It took an enormous act of will for me to seize control of my own body, to keep it from following through with the leap my nervous system had already initiated. It was a close thing, but I succeeded and kept myself still.

This isn't right, I thought, even as anger tried to further cloud my thoughts. I tried to climb on top of it. *Max is my friend. And Avery is. . .she's a friend, nothing more.* I took a deep, calming breath and slowly released it, allowing my unaccustomed rage to flow out with it. *This isn't right at all. I shouldn't be angry at all, much less this angry. Calm. Gotta stay calm.* My body slowly relaxed as I found a fragile sense of peace at last. I kept my breathing slow and even, which helped me settle back down.

Max released Avery's hand, and looked over at me. His face fell into a more serious expression.

"Kane. It is good to see you, though I wished the circumstances were better. Ariana told me about your problem," his eyes fell to my wrists, where the bone cuffs resisted any attempt of mine to veil them. "How can I help?"

Bewildered by my sudden burst of aggression, I paused to be absolutely sure I wouldn't say something stupid. When I thought I was all right, I replied as calmly as I could, "Have you ever run across a sorcerer named Malleus?"

If he noticed my behavior, he seemed to ignore it. He shook his head, "No, I have not. Ariana mentioned him, and I've no memory of such. I had my people run a search and they came up with nothing. That in itself is unusual, since my databases are extensive. May I see the cuffs?"

As I moved closer to him, my fighting instincts engaged again, in spite of my efforts to remain calm. Max was a werewolf. A predator, and a damned dangerous one. I had age and experience on my side, but he edged the scale on sheer strength and size. I've beaten bigger, many times, but Max would be a very formidable opponent. I found myself imagining how I would attack him, where I'd need to slash at his legs to hobble him, his neck so he'd bleed out quickly. My heart rate picked up and my body tensed as it readied for combat, almost before I knew what was going on. *He's my friend. He's trying to help me. Simmer down*. I stopped moving towards him, taking a few more seconds to get a handle on myself again. When I regained control, I continued. The whole thing had taken a couple of seconds at most, but I knew he'd seen it this time.

"Are you well, Kane?" Max's voice sounded concerned. He wasn't afraid of me, even if he sensed my sudden urges to attack him. He was too noble for that.

"Yes, I think," I replied slowly, "although I'm feeling a bit, um, ill-tempered at the moment." I paused, but made myself add, "I meant no offense."

"Not to worry, Kane, I'd be equally disconcerted if I found myself in your position. Indeed, I was in a similar state when we first met. I'll do anything I can to help."

Max reached out with his giant hands and lifted my own so he could get a better look at my manacles. "Hmmmm. . ." Max rumbled, "Yes, I can feel their power. They've got a dark aspect to them, to be sure." He sighed as he released my hands. He swiftly skirted the desk, where a sleek laptop awaited him. He didn't bother to sit down, but wiggled the mouse around a bit, tapped the keys, then shook his head as he examined the results on the screen. "As I thought. Those must be totally unique to that particular sorcerer. I have nothing on them."

Avery spoke up, her voice laced with concern, "What can we do? This guy's put out a contract on you, and Kane's supposed to fulfill it. Obviously, he doesn't want to do that." She glanced at me for confirmation. I blinked at her for a second before I realized she wanted me to respond.

"Right," I said.

She waited for more, but when I remained silent, she started again, "Is there anything else you can do to help us?"

Max walked back around to our side of the desk and leaned back against it, folding his arms and frowning as he considered the question. "We need to locate this. . .Malleus. Whatever grudge he has against me might be addressed financially." He sighed and ran a hand through his hair as he mused, "But then, there's no guarantee that he wouldn't just take the money and try to have me killed anyway. Honestly, I'd be happy to smooth this over if I could, but this is the first I've heard of it, and if he's jumping straight to murder-for-hire, I doubt money's going to do any good."

My words came out almost of their own volition, "Who could be holding a grudge? Is there someone you've screwed over in the past that wants payback now? Surely you've done someone dirty in the last few decades."

Ariana gasped. In retrospect, I might have been rude. "Kane!"

Max waved in dismissal, unperturbed, "It's a perfectly valid question." He paused again, thinking, then shrugged. "I'm the head of a massive corporation. I try to run it with compassion and stewardship in mind. I prefer to find situations where everybody wins as often as I can, and my people are good at creating such circumstances. That said, it's always possible that someone, somewhere, might have been dissatisfied with something the company did. But this," he nodded at my cuffs, "seems like a lot of trouble for someone to go to as a result of our business dealings. That seems unlikely." He tapped one finger on his chin, musing. "As for personal vendettas, the days of my wayward and hotheaded youth are long gone. I've grown up and tried to be respectable ever since. Anyone with whom I've had a deeply personal conflict over the centuries is dead, most of them from old age. If I dealt with them personally, then they were a danger to themselves and others. I don't kill out of spite. The last issue I had was one of our clan who went rogue and killed half of the small town in which he lived. He had no immediate family that we knew of, no children, nothing, and the people of that town expressed nothing but gratitude that justice had been served. I sincerely doubt that had anything to do with this, and the last time anything like that happened was over a hundred years ago."

"Well, someone out there seems pretty pissed off at you," I offered, "and he seems determined to get this done. I'm an assassin, not a mercenary. I'm a tool of the goddess, and not for hire. But a bargain is a bargain to the Fae. I didn't want to agree to it in the first place, but the bastard ensured that I had to, or else I'd be maimed immediately. Now we've got to either beat the solution out of him or. . ." I looked at Max, unwilling to speak further.

He nodded. "Yes, the alternatives are vastly unpleasant. For both of us." He picked his cell phone up from the desk. He thumbed it awake, placed a call, then held it to his ear. "Cheryl, yes, I'll be in Houston until the end of the week. And I need you to prepare everything for Project Demise, just in case." Max listened for a few moments, then replied, "Yes, that's right. No, it's only a precautionary measure, but you know I like to be prepared. If you don't hear from me by Saturday, then please proceed. Yes, it's been a pleasure." He thumbed the phone again and put it down. He looked up at us and smiled sadly. "Precautions, you understand. I have several artifacts that need to be handled, ah, delicately. And they need to be stored away safely in the event of my untimely passing."

I remembered that he still had the Castellata Sword, an ancient and powerful blade that had been the reason for his abduction two years ago. I wondered what else he might be holding for safekeeping.

He looked at me. "I know you don't want to hurt me, Kane. But you've made a bargain. I don't want to leave anything to chance where a GrimFaerie is concerned." To Ariana, he said, "You've got the credit cards I gave you?" She nodded. "Good. Anything you need, don't hesitate to use them." He sighed. "I want to help. I know I should have Edge fly me to Alaska to get away from you, Kane, but I'll be able to help more here. I have a couple of hunches to run down, and I'll contact Ariana the moment I find a way to assist you. Southern accent, you said?"

"Yes. Not like Edge, more syrupy. Formal sounding. Until I pissed him off, that is."

Max chuckled. "Yes, I don't doubt that you managed that, my friend." He thought for a moment before he continued, "I'll check over my business dealings in the southern areas that might be pertinent. I have a handful of enterprises in that region, but not so many that it would preclude a little digging."

"That's a start, I guess." I paused, thinking. I came to a decision. "I need to tell you that these cuffs are doing something to me. It's not good."

His eyebrows rose at that. "Oh? Like what?"

I gritted my teeth in frustration before I responded, "They seem to be. . .pushing me. Enhancing my aggression. I don't know if it's specific to you or if it's more general, but I nearly attacked you a couple of times since we've been here. It was a close thing. I don't like that." Both Ariana and Avery gasped at that revelation but remained quiet for the time being.

Max nodded and slipped his hands into his pockets, unconsciously demonstrating his lack of concern. "Hmmm, yes, I felt that from you, those bursts of intense aggression. And your restraint as well, which is impressive, my friend." He smiled, "and I'm not afraid to say I'm glad of that." He looked at each of the women in the room, then addressed us all. "We'll just have to get this figured out as quickly as possible." He briefly stayed silent, then picked up his cellphone again and thumbed at it for several seconds. "There's one person here in town that I think might be able to help us."

Ariana jumped in. "Really? Who is it? Where can we find them?"

Max looked up at her. "Cyrus McLeod. He runs an occult shop downtown, 'Bell, Book, and Cauldron'. Have you been there?"

Ariana laughed. "Of course, any witch within a hundred miles has been there. Old Cyrus is like the

Amazon of occult stuff hereabouts. If you need it, he can probably find it."

I knew the man. For a human, Cyrus McLeod was old when I'd met him two decades ago. He hid behind the persona of a new age store owner who was more interested in selling his wares than in the secrets of the universe. But I'd seen his aura, and I knew he'd done and seen some things that had changed him. He wasn't Fae, but that was about all I knew for certain about the guy. The full extent of his powers was unknown to me, but he had a deep well of knowledge to draw from, so I'd always assumed he could throw down if necessary. It's never the big, tough-talking guys I kept an eye on. No, the normal-looking people with intelligence and intense focus, those were the ones who end up causing me trouble. Muscle was cheap, discipline was dangerous. And I knew Cyrus had the latter.

I nodded slowly. "I know Cyrus." I sighed before adding, "And he knows me." I shook my head slowly and a rueful grin almost made it to one side of my mouth. "I don't think he'll be pleased to see us, but let's get on with it."

Ariana chimed in, "I can have us there in a half-hour, no problem. How can he help, Max?"

Max folded his arms, his biceps bulging against the fabric of his tailored shirt as he did so. "Cyrus has helped me in the past. He has some tracking spells that are far more refined than most." He nodded in my direction, "If anyone could get a bearing on the maker of those cuffs, I think Cyrus can. It's not much, but it's more than you've got now."

Avery spoke up, "Is there anything else we could be doing right now? Anything specific we should ask this Cyrus?" Her voice unexpectedly twanged something in me. I liked it. I liked it a lot. I squeezed my eyes shut and forced myself to relax yet again. The cuffs seemed to be amping me up in more ways than one.

Ignoring my struggle, Max shook his head, "No, but if I think of anything at all, you know I'll call you right away. I wish I had something more concrete, but this Malleus is a bit of a mystery." He stepped away from the desk and brought himself to his full height, "Let's see if we can unravel him, shall we? Go see Cyrus. Let me know what he says. I'll keep running down leads as best I can."

Ariana leapt over to him and he bent to accept a quick kiss from her before she turned for the door. Avery followed her, but I lingered for a moment. Max met my eyes as he awaited my next words. I paused until the girls had made it into the next room before I spoke.

"You should probably avoid me until this is done."

Max leaned back on his desk again and nodded, his face displaying nothing but open honesty. "I plan to do exactly that."

"You're afraid of me?" The words were out of my mouth before I knew it. My predatory self was trying to claw its way out at every turn, it seemed.

Max sighed. "Absolutely. You're a GrimFaerie, one of the most dangerous of your kind. You've spent centuries stalking and killing bigger game than werewolves, even one such as me. I am what I am, but I don't care about who would be the winner, Kane. My ego doesn't need me to talk about how tough I am. I'm far more concerned that one or both of us would either be gravely injured or killed if we were to fight. Even if only one of us died, I don't want it to be you," he grinned with genuine humor, "and I damned well don't want it to be me either. I'll happily stay out of your way and help as much as I possibly can, for both our sakes. Goddess be with you, Kane. Keep me posted."

Chapter 5

Bell, Book, and Cauldron had moved a few times over the years, and its current incarnation occupied a wide, brown building on Montrose Boulevard not far from downtown. Only a couple of cars sat in the lot, one of which I'd hardly call a car. The color and size of a large apple, I recognized it as a 'Smart Car' supposedly quite fuel efficient. That might have been perfectly true, but I didn't like the idea of driving something I could have just as easily thrown. Granted, motorcycles were even smaller, but definitely more fun to drive.

It was nearly closing time according to the sign on the door, which suited us just fine. A tiny bell tinkled brightly to announce our entrance, and once inside, we were assailed by the smells of incense, sandalwood, and old books. Rows of shelves displaying all kinds of occult materials surrounded us. To our left, I saw a locked cabinet filled with crystal balls, detailed dragon figurines, and some very stout and old-looking leatherbound books. Beyond the glass cabinet, we saw sections devoted to newer books, carefully labeled herbs and crystals, as well as an impressive rack of iron cauldrons of various sizes. Some of my kin would stay away from those, being intensely affected by iron. I had a certain level of immunity to it, though I never asked why. Probably a perk of my job.

Jewelry and clothing dominated the right side of the store, along with displays of framed artwork. The wall facing us was covered with swords and axes of sufficient variety that they made me smile. Some appeared to be cheaply made novelties, but I picked out a quite a few combat-ready weapons among the stock that looked like serious fun to me.

A long octagonal cabinet sat in the middle of the floor, constructed with a central space large enough to allow a clerk to stand. Inside that wood and glass fortress, a young woman with purple hair, a glittering nose ring and black accented makeup was leaning on the countertop, talking to a young man with thick glasses, a scraggly brown beard, and ear gauges that I could have stuck my thumb through. The girl was going over the differences between two tarot decks and the young man was pretending to listen intently while ogling the generous amount of cleavage protruding from the clerk's clingy t-shirt.

She threw a glance our way, caught my eye and said, "Be with you guys in a sec." Her gaze lingered for a moment, and I felt a sudden, fierce pang of arousal, a lusty hunger that I knew exactly how to sate. I took a step towards the clerk and halted.

Many of the Faerie indulged every whim, every fleeting desire. That was their prerogative, I guess. As for me, I had a job to do, and if I wanted to do it well, I had to rein that shit in. Unlike my kin, I've never taken a woman, human or otherwise, without her consent. I had rules. I've never done that. I could use magick to make a woman want me so badly that they'd kill to have me. In fact, I've used that power many times over the centuries in my line of work to get close to a target, but I've never desired to complete the act. I simply implanted a false memory of the best (or worst) night of their life, depending on the situation. I lived by my own code, and I did it my own way.

By that same token, just because someone flashes their cleavage and a come-hither smile, that meant nothing to me. Often, those were nothing more than traps. Although my libido ran as high as that of any Fae, I still chose. I was the one who controlled how I dealt with my needs, so I intensely disliked being manipulated through them.

At the moment, I thought of nothing but the thinness of the clerk's t-shirt and how I wanted to see what was barely hidden underneath it. I knew my claws could part the waistband of her jeans quite easily. My blood sang, my heart raced, and I recognized how close I was to being out of control.

I slammed an iron fist down on those urges. I clenched my teeth and took a deep breath as I forced discipline onto my raging thoughts and quelled my body's unconscious responses.

This isn't me, I thought. *It's got to be Malleus. Damn him.*

"Hey," Ariana whispered, "did you growl just now?" Surprise suffused her quiet words. My behavior had not escaped her notice, and I could tell it worried her. At her side, Avery looked likewise concerned.

"Probably," I sighed, focusing on my breathing until I was calmer. "These cuffs are pushing me. It's not good." Malleus said he'd attached an enhancer spell to the cuffs, something to increase my overall aggression. He wanted to be sure that I'd get the job done with Max. The problem was that my libido saddled up for the ride. Even Ariana was starting to look good to me and that's never how I thought of her. Ever. And I carefully avoided looking at Avery.

The girl swiped the young man's card then handed it back along with a bag, throwing him a brilliant smile that made his cheeks redden. Distracted, he somehow made it past us without stumbling and the young woman turned our way, unconsciously posing with one hand on her shapely hip. "Now, how can I help you?"

She still looked good enough to eat. I was glad the huge glass case separated us. I was maintaining control, but I must have taken too long to speak, because Avery stepped forward.

Moving with calm authority, Avery produced her badge and showed it to the girl. When she spoke, her voice possessed a firm, self-assured tone: strong, yet melodic and feminine. I liked it. "Detective Avery Lynne, Harris County Sherrif's office. We need to talk to Cyrus MacLeod. Where is he?"

Surprised, the girl put her fingers to her lips as if to stifle a gasp, then shot a glance over her shoulder. "Cyrus? Um...he's in the back. Is he in trouble?"

Avery shook her head. "No, not at all. We'd just like to ask him some questions." She waited a beat before continuing. "Will you take us to him, please?"

Purple hair's eyes went round, "Oh! Yes, um, follow me, please." She unfolded the board that allowed her to exit the display and gently let it fall back into place. "Right this way." She gestured and walked towards a doorway in the back. We followed her into a short corridor with a few doors on either side and one larger door at the end of the hall. "Bathrooms are there," she pointed, "and Cyrus should be in his office there. Just go on in, he usually loves visitors. Cyrus! Detective to see you!" She raised her voice then lowered it once more, "Y'all need anything, let me know, I'm starting the evening cleaning before we close." Her eyes locked with mine for a moment and I felt her breath catch in her throat. She felt me. *Dammit.*

"Thank you." Avery's interruption distracted me and gave the girl a chance to extricate herself. When she was gone, I stayed silent. I had to figure out how to calm down before things got even more problematic than they already were. I looked down at the cuffs and stifled another growl, this time of frustration.

Ariana stepped forward to knock on the door but before her knuckles made contact, the latch opened, and the door swung inwards of its own volition. I detected the faintest tingle of magick in the air, as I'm sure Ariana and Avery did.

"Come in, my friends," an elderly voice wheezed, thin and shaky, and burring with a slight Scottish brogue. "Yes, yes, come in and see old Cyrus."

We entered the room and found ourselves in a cozy office, crammed full of books, statues, and various occult paraphernalia. It was busy but gave the impression of carefully organized chaos. Everything had its place, there was just a lot of everything. Looking at some of the neater stacks, I hoped Ariana would take notes. She must have guessed my thoughts, because she narrowed her eyes and stuck her tongue out at me.

Cyrus sat behind a large wooden desk that looked a century old. His gaze shifted back and forth between the page in his hand and something on one of the two computer monitors that sat on one corner of the desk. He quickly laid the paper down, jotted a note on it, then filed it in a manila folder without ever looking up at us.

A tall and slender man, Cyrus was pale and wrinkled with age. A tuft of white hair encircled his bald head, matching a wispy white goatee that lent the impression of a mountain goat. His eyes rose from his work and he regarded us for a moment, squinting. With a shaky hand, he affixed a pair of gold-rimmed glasses atop a prominent nose. His vision thus enhanced, he looked at us each in turn. He nodded in recognition at Ariana but cocked his head to one side as he examined Avery, looking as though he wasn't quite sure what to make of her. Then his eyes moved to me.

Moving far quicker than a man of his apparent age should be able, he shoved himself out of his seat. He yanked open a drawer to grab a handgun of impressive size, a nickel-plated automatic of some kind, and pointed it at me even as he produced a foot-long wand from somewhere with his other hand. The carved wood was as thick as my thumb, glowing with an intense golden light. I recognized the weapon, a wand specifically attuned to Cyrus's magick. It would blast me across the room if I let it.

"YOU!" he barked in a voice far stronger and younger than the one he'd greeted us with. Gone was the doddering old scholar-merchant. This was a faded warrior, a sorcerer who knew his game, and I'd pissed him off without saying a word. "Get out of here, Grim! I've done nothing whatsoever to warrant a visit from you! Nothing!"

Avery and Ariana started yelling, pointing their own guns at Cyrus. It wasn't helping. I'd crouched in preparation to attack, but dammit, I was tired of being pushed around by whatever spell Malleus had applied to the cuffs. I knew why Cyrus was upset. And I knew what I could do to calm things down. I just didn't like it.

Using every bit of strength and control I could find, I forced myself to stand up straight as I eased my hands over my head.

Gritting my teeth, I growled, "Cyrus, I'm not here for you. You're safe from me. We need your help. And—" I hated to say it, "—and I'm sorry about your car. I mean it. I apologize. Formally." I paused and added a bit in Scots Gaelic, just to be sure it would sink in. I was a little rusty, but I think I got my point across.

Cyrus froze in place and his eyes went wide with shock. His weapons lowered a tiny fraction. "Say that again."

I closed my eyes and switched back to English. "I said I'm sorry, Cyrus. I shouldn't have thrown your car at that demon. My bad."

Cyrus gaped at me for a few seconds, then his expression shifted into something resembling hurt rather than fury, though his weapons remained ready. "I loved that car, and you knew it."

"I needed to kill that demon before it got away. There were kids in the house next door. It was the best I could do." I gritted my teeth, "I'm sorry."

"Kids?" Cyrus lowered the gun to his side and the wand's glow disappeared. "I didn't know there were kids in there."

"My hearing is better than yours."

Cyrus sighed and nodded. "So it is. It is, indeed." He digested this information for a moment, frowning, but then he laughed. A mere chuckle at first, he really got after it once he got going, laughing so hard I thought he'd have a stroke. He kept laughing as he made his way back to his desk, ignoring Ariana and Avery's drawn guns completely. He put his own gun back in its drawer and laid the wand out of the way on the desktop as he reseated himself. Tears formed in his eyes, and he dabbed at them with a kerchief as he regained his composure. Relieved, I lowered my hands.

"My stars," he said once he could speak again, "Of all the things I didn't expect today, that was top o' the list. Imagine! A GrimFaerie. . .*apologizing*! Och, I never heard the like." To me, he nodded graciously, his eyes atwinkle, "Master Kane, your apology is accepted. I bought a better car anyway, a wee red thing. Truth be told, that whole thing was my fault in the first place. Now then, what can I do for you?"

Avery and Ariana looked at each other briefly, then reluctantly holstered their weapons. Avery glanced at me and half-smiled. "You threw—?"

"His car, yes. At a demon." I rolled my eyes. "Look, it was the only weapon I could find, and it worked. Those VW Beetles are funny-looking anyway."

"Hey, now!" Cyrus tried to protest, but the rebuke held no heat. "That old blue car was loyal and trustworthy. We'd been through a lot together and I liked it!"

I introduced Ariana and Avery, and Cyrus made himself charming as always. He remembered Ariana, though it had been a while since they'd spoken, and he fawned over Avery something awful. This time, I was more prepared for the surge of jealousy kindled by the cuffs and kept my cool. Mostly.

Once the pleasantries were over, I held out my forearms so he could see my problem. "We could use your help. I've been forced into an agreement by a sorcerer named Malleus. He made these cuffs, which'll do nasty things to me if I don't get his job done by midnight tonight. Can you tell us anything about them? How to remove them? Or maybe where Malleus might be?"

Behind his glasses, Cyrus squinted at the bands around my wrists and he perked up. "Oh! Oh, let me have a look at those, if you please." He cleared the folders and a few other items from his desk for me and I laid my forearms in front of him, palms up so he could examine them. Cyrus leaned down to inspect the bone manacles, pulled a pencil from a nearby mug full of them and tapped the cuffs gently with its sharpened tip. There was a tiny greenish spark each time he made contact. "Gracious, a lot of power went into these. A lot of it. This fellow's no slouch, I can tell you that." He looked up at me, his eyes twinkling with curiosity behind his lenses. "What's his name again? Malleus?"

"Yes, that's what he said. I didn't see his face, but he sounded like he was from the deep South."

Cyrus wrinkled his nose at that but said nothing. He bent to look at the cuffs for a few moments longer before he pulled up his chair and relaxed into it. "Let me see how I can put this." He waited a beat before delivering the news. "You're screwed."

As if those were magick words, things went right to shit.

Chapter 6

A woman's scream pierced the office walls, jolting all of us to our feet. A crash followed, along with the sharp sound of breaking glass. Nothing good ever came from such sounds.

"Lorena!" Cyrus called as he bolted from his seat, snatching his weapons from the desk as he rushed towards the door. I yanked the door open, Ariana and Avery close behind, weapons ready.

We rushed through the short hallway and back into the main area of the store, where only half the lights still worked, illuminating a scene of destruction. The tall glass cabinet near the door had toppled, strewing its contents across the floor to mingle with a thousand glass shards. The shop girl screamed again, drawing our attention to our right, where the taller bookcases stood. She cowered there, crammed into a corner, struggling to make herself as small as possible. A demon stood in the midst of the debris.

Standing around seven feet tall, its overlong arms hung at its sides, its ghastly hands tipped with sharp claws. Although not a thickly built beast, I knew from experience that its ropy muscles were strong as steel cables. Dirty white skin, pebbled and warty like a toad's, covered its hideous body. Its face looked like something that had melted in the sun, its hooded eyes glowing yellow from deep within their sockets. It turned my way and uttered a malevolent growl, then dismissed me and took a step towards the terrified girl in the corner.

Without missing a beat, Ariana opened fire. In an eyeblink, she dropped to one knee, took aim with both of her handguns, and methodically emptied both magazines into the creature's torso. Ariana's magickal rounds thwacked into its flesh, each impact flaring brightly. The demon surprised me by not going down. Ariana's specially-made kills-everything rounds had always been effective against demons, but this one stayed on its feet. Even so, the bullets must have hurt it, as it halted and ran a clawed hand over the wounds as if surveying the damage.

Seizing the moment, I dashed over to the girl and scooped her up. She clutched at my neck in terror, which made my job easier, and she felt light as a feather. Soft though. In all the right places. *Focus!* I reminded myself as I leapt back to the relative shelter of the hallway with my friends. I set Lorena down on her feet and shoved her towards safety.

"Get in my office and bolt the door! Quickly, lass!" Cyrus directed, but she was already halfway down the hall, her eyes wide with fright. Cyrus caught my eye and nodded a thank you. I ignored him—we had work to do. He readied his weapons and edged his way in between Ariana and Avery, looking for a shot.

The creature bellowed in rage and raised its two enormous fists high over its head and brought them down on the store's octagonal display case with a crash.

"Not me cabinet, ye cockwobble!" Cyrus yelled. Furious, he unleashed a bolt of golden energy from his wand. It struck the demon's chest hard enough to back it up a step, scorching its skin. It howled in pain, but then regained its balance. As we watched, its wounds closed and healed themselves. Cyrus fired his automatic as well, but barely annoyed the beast.

"My turn," Avery said, her voice tight. I felt her magick awaken, an intense vibration that emanated from her core. It washed over me, through me, and I have to say, it felt good. Her body took on a faint bluish glow in the dim light. She shone brighter with each passing moment as she focused on her power, gathering it within herself. Suddenly, the light flowed down her arms, and her gun glowed as she poured magick into it. The bullets that emerged from the barrel left white-hot trails of energy as they screamed across the short space that separated her from the demon. They impacted in its misshapen head and face, rocking it back as it wailed in agony. I thought it would go down. I knew from experience that Avery's magick-infused bullets carried an incredible kick, potent against supernatural beings. It clutched its shattered face and went down to a knee, moaning in agony.

It lurched to its feet again and loosed a bestial cry of rage that I found myself returning in kind. It snatched up a piece of debris, a jagged hunk of wood and glass, and flung it at Avery.

That, my friends, made me angry. Like, "seeing red" angry.

I leaped in front of Avery and hit the flying wreckage with my body, deflecting the worst of it. Glass sliced open my shoulder, and I welcomed that sweet, sharp agony. It woke me up. Something on the wall caught my eye and I lashed out with one hand to snatch it up. The double-bitted battle axe wasn't for show like some of the other weapons, and it carried a razor edge. Thus armed, I launched myself at the demon, already swinging the axe as I covered the distance.

The demon roared and raised an arm up to shield itself from my attack. The blade hammered into its forearm bones, sinking deeply. It howled in pain but retaliated before I could yank the axe away and hit it again. Its huge, bony fist slammed into my chest and face, and I staggered back a step, losing my grip on the haft of the axe. It reached up and grabbed the handle, yanked the axe out of its arm and discarded it before swinging its open hands at me, talons gleaming. The first hit me before I was ready, and I took a handful of bloody gashes across my chest as I flinched backwards, but I recovered enough to duck the thing's second clumsy attack. Using every bit of coiled strength in my legs, I sprang forward and hit the creature just above its knobby knees with everything I had. Bingo. It grunted in surprise and toppled over onto its back, landing amidst more shards of wood and glass, and it yowled in pain. I monkeyed up its torso to straddle its midsection. It reached an enormous hand towards me, claws extended.

I swiped its arm out of the way to show it what my own claws could do.

To be honest, I don't remember much from the next several seconds. A wave of anger overtook me as I went along for the ride, unleashing all my pent-up frustrations and arousal with each swipe of my claws. Ripping. Tearing. Nothing else mattered. Wet blood on my arms. Cracking of bones. Rage and violence. Bliss.

"Kane! Kane, stop! It's dead already, stop it!"

Avery's voice sounded so far away at first, but it penetrated the haze in my mind. It touched whatever there is in me to call a heart. The sound of her voice, beautiful and pleading, I couldn't deny it. The sound of it brought me back from wherever I'd gone. I blinked my eyes a few times and the store came back into focus. I heard my own labored breathing echoing in the relative stillness. I looked over my shoulder and saw three pairs of wide eyes staring back at me. Avery's face, so striking and elegant, revealed her fear. My brain came back online, and I realized that it was me, not the demon, that inspired that look.

At the thought of the beast, I looked down and saw what remained it, which was not much. It resembled something recently run through an industrial strength woodchipper. Twice. *No wonder my shoulders feel tired,* I thought. I sighed, making sure I was under control before I looked back at my friends.

59

Scaring humans was part of my job. I use fear as just another tool, and it's one of my favorites. But seeing Ariana and Avery look at me like that—that was different. And I didn't like it.

Malleus, you bastard, what have you done to me?

"Are you all right?" Avery's blue-green eyes shone with concern. It's not something I'm used to seeing. In a way, seeing fear in them was easier.

"Yes," I said, coming up to my feet. I looked at my hands, grimaced at what I saw there, and grabbed up a fallen scarf to wipe the gore from my arms. "It's another lesser demon. Apparently, Malleus knows we're here."

The corpse of the lesser demon burst into soundless black flames that covered every inch of its body, quickly dissolving it away. From within the silent fire, a faint, emerald green radiance seeped from the demon, a wispy cloud that moved as if alive. It snaked through the air and came together in a rough sphere that hovered a few feet above the floor. A smooth, syrupy-sweet voice emanated from it, and I wrinkled up my nose in disgust.

"Well, well, you seem to have forgotten that your time is limited," the disembodied voice of Malleus drawled. "You passed up one chance already. You really should get to work, don't you think?"

Blinding pain erupted from my wrists, driving me to my knees. Searing, burning agony assailed me, forcing my fingers to curl and clench in spasms. I couldn't speak. Animal grunts escaped me as slender rivulets of blood ran from beneath the bone manacles to patter on the floor.

"It'll only be worse for you if you don't come through. Stop dilly-dallying and do as you're told, Grim."

Before anyone could say anything else, the cloud vanished without a trace, taking the cursed voice of Malleus with it, and letting a heavy silence fall over the store.

"That. . .that *bastard*," Cyrus fumed. He looked over the wreckage of his store before focusing on me again. "Dammit, I knew you'd be trouble, Grim. Look at this mess!" He waved his hands furiously at the shattered wreckage of his shop.

"We'll reimburse you for the damages," Ariana offered. "We can pay right now. Plus extra for the inconvenience, and there are some things we'll probably need. If you'll help us, that is. I assume you take credit cards?" She slipped a gleaming black card from one of her pockets, a wolfshead logo flashing in gold on the front. "Oh, and Max says hi."

Cyrus caught sight of the card and recognized it. He froze in mid-rant while the merchant in him did something of a backflip. His smile returned and his manner cheered substantially.

"Oh, he does? Please convey my greetings as well. I do, indeed, take credit cards, lass. Take whatever you like, I'll total everything up."

Chapter 7

Cyrus helped us carry the boxes outside. Considering how much money we'd paid him, I was surprised he didn't offer to wash the Jeep while we were there. He'd spent a few minutes with the clerk, Lorena, making sure she was unharmed, and she surprised us all by expressing excitement rather than fear to discover that the supernatural world truly existed. Humans could be remarkably resilient sometimes. The girl promptly asked for a hazard bonus, which she got in return for her vow of silence regarding the whole incident. She set about tidying up the wreckage while Cyrus aided us.

He pulled out two business cards and handed them to Ariana and Avery, who tucked them away. He bowed to Ariana, who'd paid for everything and then some. "Pleasure doing business with you. If either of you need anything else, don't hesitate to call me."

Avery replied, "Any info you might have on Malleus's identity might be nice."

Cyrus nodded and scratched his chin. "Only one of my customers comes to mind," he offered. "Someone moved into the old Worthington place in the Heights late last year. At least, that's the address they used when they started ordering from us online, and I heard a few vague rumors. I remember because a lot of the items they ordered were hard to get and some were quite exotic. Expensive, you understand."

"You haven't been selling anything. . .?" Avery spoke up, her cop instincts on alert.

Cyrus shook his head, "No, I steadfastly refuse to sell anything illegal or designated strictly off-limits by the Assembly. I sell nothing for necromancy or evil magick here." He sighed, "That said, almost anything can be used for either good or evil. It's the intent of the practitioner and the specific combinations of items that turns it either way."

Avery turned to Ariana, "The Assembly?"

Ariana arranged the last box in the Jeep's cargo area and slammed the tailgate shut. "They're kind of the governing body for the magickal community. It's a pretty loose outfit, but it means well. They do have some stiff penalties for evil magick but getting them to stick is another thing altogether. Plus, there's never an Enforcer around when you need one." Ariana cocked a thumb over her shoulder at me. "I suspect that's why GrimFaeries do what they do. Bad guys know it, too. The Grims are the real reason folks avoid magick that hurts others."

Avery's eyes focused on me and I held her gaze. "You're a police officer. Aren't you?" There was an understanding in her voice that thrilled me all the way to my toes. But it scared me, too. I looked away.

"I'm an assassin," I corrected her, keeping my tone as icy as possible. "That's all I've ever been. I kill whomever I'm assigned to kill. There's nothing noble about it."

Avery didn't let it go.

"Every single kill has been someone or something evil. Like Tanya Thornwall. Even," she paused to take a breath, "my grandfather. Am I right?"

I didn't answer. That was my business. At least, that's what I told myself. But she was right. Tanya Thornwall had been a murdering sorceress, aspiring to become a Skinwalker. She'd used drugs to allow demons to possess innocent people, through whom they committed violence and nearly killed others. She even sent a demon to kill her own mother, and that was after the Goddess herself had put me on her trail. When I figured out who and what she was, it was obvious that she'd never stop, and needed to be put down, so to speak. For the greater good.

It had always been like that for me. For centuries, I'd get visions, glimpses of places and people, and the knowledge that I needed to move on them. My job was to find out who was doing dirty deeds and stop them, which usually meant killing them. Even so, I worked for the Light. So, I was a good guy. Right? So why was I pushing Avery away? We were the same, she and I. I didn't know if it was the enchantment of the cuffs that made my heart beat harder when she came near or if it was something in me that felt a connection to her, but the distinction didn't really matter. I didn't need to get involved like that with anyone, especially not a human. It would slow me down, and I couldn't afford that. *But what if. . .? No. No way. Stop it.* My thoughts battled each other like that for several seconds before I finally shut them down.

"Whatever," I answered. I ignored the hurt that flitted across her face and turned back to Cyrus. "Can you get us that address?"

Cyrus's face broke into a wide grin. "I'm nothing if not organized. I'll print the invoices up for you right now, you'll have the address and a detailed list of everything he ordered. If he is behind all this, I hope he gets what's coming to him."

"Oh, he will. You can count on that." And then a particularly nasty realization forced its way into my thick skull. It took shape for a few seconds, bringing my fury back to a boil. "Sohn einer Hündin!" I hissed, clenching my fists in frustration. "Gaaahh!"

"What the hell, Kane?" Ariana came around and eyed me with concern. "We just need the address and then we'll be ready to move out."

I got my anger under control, shook my head, and uttered words I could barely believe. "I can't go with you."

Ariana's mouth dropped open, but Avery gasped as she figured it out. Smart, that one.

64

"He's tracking you with the cuffs! That's how he knew you'd seen Max and not killed him and how he knew we were here. He's got you LoJacked."

My sudden confusion dulled my rage. I blinked at the reference and glanced at Ariana for an explanation.

"It's a device used to track stolen cars, Kane."

"Ah," I nodded. "Yes, then. LoJacked. Bastard knows where I am. He's linked to the cuffs. I don't know how much he can see and hear, but it's enough to let him know we were close to Max. Damn him! I'm gonna rip his spine out through his mouth when I get my claws on him."

Ariana smiled and I detected a certain devious set to her lips. "I might just know a way to kill two birds with one stone." She looked at Cyrus and turned on her charm, "Cyrus, dear, do you have a conjuring room here? A protected circle?"

Cyrus smiled and bowed deeply. "My lady, what kind of wizard would I be if I didn't? You're planning to cut the link, I presume?" She nodded, and he smiled, "'Follow me, please."

We locked up the Jeep and followed Cyrus through the wreckage of the store, down the hall, and into his office. He pushed a button on the underside of his desk and one of the bookcases popped away from the wall. He swung it all the way open and stepped inside the concealed room, flipping the light on as he did so. We followed him in.

Cyrus's conjuring room looked far bigger than his office. Cabinets and bookshelves covered the windowless walls, everything carefully ordered and labeled. A long worktable ran along one wall, bearing a wide array of vials, beakers, and other implements common to botany, chemistry, and alchemy. Again, everything existed in a neat and tidy arrangement.

A ten-foot diameter pentacle, inlaid with gold and copper wire, lay embedded in the smooth, hardwood floor. Three concentric circles surrounded the usual five-pointed star, with eldritch symbols carefully inscribed between them. I knew without looking that the top of the star pointed northward, as did those of most wizards that stayed on the Goddess's good side. These days, those who had theirs pointed southward used it as a means of focusing ill intent. The symbol didn't start out that way, but things change over the centuries, and it's not the symbol that's meaningful anyway; it's the will of the user that truly makes the difference.

"Kane, stand in the middle, please." Ariana directed, all business now. "Cyrus, do you have malachite? And white quartz crystals?"

"You wound me, madam," Cyrus feigned outrage, but laughed. "This is an occult shop. Of course, I do. I'll be right back."

I stood in the center of the circles as directed. "What's your plan?"

Cyrus shuffled back in carrying a box that rattled as he moved. He presented it to Ariana, who thanked him and took the box. "Oooh, these are nice!" she exclaimed, holding one of the chunks of green stone up to the light.

"Only the best from my shop, my dear," Cyrus assured her.

Ariana placed the greenish stones along with a chunk of clear quartz crystal around the circle at every point of intersection with the inscribed star. Once she had finished, she stepped back to admire her handiwork. Satisfied, she looked back up to me and realized I'd asked her a question. "Oh, right. I'm going to cast a protection spell around you that I'm hoping will kill his ability to track you. If I'm right, there's a magickal thread connecting those cuffs, and you, to our guy Malleus. I can't do anything about the original enchantment he put on the cuffs, but I'm pretty sure I can cut that thread so he can't spy on you anymore." A sly grin appeared on her face. "And I'm going to throw a little shock his way as a surprise!" She looked over at Avery. "I'm going to need your magickal muscle here. I can get this done by myself, but with you helping, the spell will pack a big enough punch that it might even give that asshole a black eye, so to speak."

Avery looked concerned but glanced at me and agreed. "Yes, of course. Anything to help. What do I have to do?"

Ariana faced me as she positioned herself in front of the circle and motioned for Avery to step closer. "Here, put your hand on my shoulder. Remember your exercises? Focus on your magick and gather it inside you. When I give you the signal, imagine it flowing down your arm and into me. I'll do the rest."

Avery nodded firmly. "Got it. I can do that." She turned those sea green eyes on me. "Are you ready, Kane?"

"Do it," I answered, steeling myself for the spell. I took a deep breath and let it out, seeking a calm that served me far better than my rage. It took a few moments, but I found it, and waited for Ariana to start the spell.

Ariana nodded and said, "Here goes. . ." She raised her hands and closed her eyes. I knew she was gathering her will, awakening the magick within her. That power is everywhere, but not many could feel it or manipulate it, and only a handful had the training and discipline to use it the way Ariana could. I felt her power blossoming inside her as she focused it in preparation for the casting of the circle.

Avery put her left hand on Ariana's right shoulder and closed her own eyes as she awakened that same energy within herself. I felt it ignite in her from ten feet away, just as I had Ariana's, but Avery's was different. The woman was *strong*. If Ariana's power was a torch, Avery's was a bonfire. I shook my head in admiration and was glad Ariana was training her. She'd be a danger to everyone around her otherwise.

Ariana stepped forward and knelt, and Avery moved in tandem with her. Ariana murmured a string of syllables I recognized as her own invocation, and she reached out and touched the wire of the circle in the floor with one finger. Power poured from her at the contact, flowing into the designs in the floor, creating a buzzing field of energy, a half-dome that completely surrounded me.

As it snapped into place, something in the room fell away, a faint sensation of pressure released, and I knew it had to be Malleus's tracking spell. The circle had cut it off, along with any other magick from outside the barrier. I smiled. *Take that, you bastard.*

Ariana moved back to her original position, still chanting, her arms up and her palms facing me as she kept control of the circle and assessed the situation. Her chant changed, the tone harsher, more clipped. I could tell she was shifting from protective magick to an offensive strike. Unfortunately, all I could do from inside the circle was watch and hope for the best. I held my breath.

Ariana's voice rose and she lashed out with her left hand in a quick snatching motion. She grabbed hold with her other hand, and a misty tendril of energy became visible, leading up and into the ceiling. It was an ugly, sickly green color, a thing born of ill magick.

Ariana grunted with the effort of hanging onto the squirming thread. She hissed a few more words in old Gaelic then gritted, "Now!" at Avery through clenched teeth.

The dome of protective energy Ariana had wrought around me kept me from feeling Avery's energy as I had before. No matter, though. I could see it. Avery's body suffused with that same blue-white light, its brightness radiating from her torso. As I watched, the glow intensified, raced through her arm and into Ariana, who yelled a final word of casting as she sent their combined energy surging through the twisting tendril.

I didn't expect the explosion.

The flash blinded me for a second or two, and I felt the circle dissipate as Ariana's focus was broken. When my eyes cleared, the sight stunned me. Everyone else in the room lay flat on their backs, unmoving. Papers floated to the floor from the explosion and I could tell that any mobile furniture in the room had been thrown aside.

I dashed over and knelt beside Ariana. There were no wounds, but her eyes were closed, and she was completely still. I cradled her head and lifted her body up so she rested in my lap.

"Ariana! Are you all right?"

She didn't answer. A trickle of blood ran down her face from a tiny cut on her forehead, and I wiped it away. She looked so young like that, so vulnerable. She took a slow breath, and then another, reassuring me that she was only unconscious. Even so, I'd seen her recover faster from worse. Considering our situation, I decided to take the liberty of entering her mind to check on her. Any other day, I'd never do that without permission, but I figured she wouldn't be too upset under the circumstances. As I'd done with hundreds, if not thousands, of humans in my long lifetime, I delved into her mind with my magick.

That is, I tried to.

Something closed off Ariana's mind so effectively I couldn't find a way in. I tried again but got the same result. Whatever had happened to her had rendered her immune to my mental magick.

"That's not good," I muttered.

"What?" Avery groaned as she sat up. She held one hand to her head as if keeping it together but otherwise seemed to be in one piece. "What's wrong? Is she ok?"

"I can't reach her," I said, barely noticing I'd whispered. "He's done something to her, that bastard." Rage tried to boil up inside me, pushed by whatever power remained in the cuffs, but to my surprise, it wouldn't come. Sadness swallowed it up. I held my friend a little closer, willing her to open her eyes. They stayed closed. I held her like that for a few seconds, and whatever you might think, I wasn't crying.

Cyrus came over and knelt beside Ariana. He checked her pulse and nodded, "She's out cold, but she seems alive and well. I don't know what Malleus did to her, but the thread that connected your cuffs to him and allowed him to spy on you has been broken. It was visible for a moment, but it disintegrated when she and Avery threw their power into it. It's gone now, but the backlash must have been enormous." He resettled his glasses on his nose. "I must say, that was an ingenious spell she cast. She wove a protection over you, a severing spell to cut Malleus off from the cuffs, and then threw an attack his way on top of it. That's pretty intricate stuff, especially not knowing the exact structure of Malleus's work. I'm slick, sir, but she put that together much faster than I expected possible."

"Are you slick enough to bring her back?" I asked, my anger gaining traction over my sadness. I wanted Malleus to pay before, but this—hurting my friends—increased the payback I owed him tenfold.

Cyrus sighed. "I don't know, Kane. I'm not sure exactly what's wrong with her yet. At the very least, I can keep her safe while I research the problem. I haven't needed to enable my stronger wards in years, but once

70

they're up, not even you could get in here. If I can find a way to help her, I surely will." He glanced at Ariana, concern etched on his worn face. "She's a sweet kid. I'll do my best."

I laid Ariana down, resting her head on a folded blanket Cyrus produced. I dug in the pockets of her cargo pants and found the keys to the Jeep. I looked at Cyrus and he handed me the invoice he'd printed. He'd circled the name and address at the top of the first page and stapled a map to it. I nodded my thanks, then forced myself to look at Avery. I found her staring intently at me with those gorgeous eyes, her face stern and ready. I waited until I was sure my voice wouldn't shake with either sadness or rage, and I spoke.

"That leaves us, then. You and me. I say we run him down and make him pay. Are you in?"

Avery set her jaw and nodded. Her voice dropped into a low, husky register when she spoke, sexy as hell. She meant business. "Hell, yes. That asshole's gonna wish he'd never been born."

Chapter 8

The ride to the Heights didn't take long. I cast a veil over the Jeep to hide us from Malleus's scrying magick, but not from the naked eye. I didn't want some fool to sideswipe us because we were too hard to see. Avery drove, as I'm not fond of the task, and I did my best to watch the road as well as the surrounding airspace. I'd been attacked by gargoyles many times, and they loved to swoop out of the night sky. If Malleus had any on his payroll, they'd think nothing of upending the car to get to us. So far, the night stayed quiet, with no sign of the flying stone creatures, or anything else that might assail us.

"We'll be there in about five minutes," Avery said, her voice low. The intensity in her words hit me immediately, a steel cord of determination surrounded by a silken purr. In the quiet, close confines of the Jeep, her voice was a physical thing that touched me, caressed me. It was good. It made me want to do things. I closed my eyes and saw my hands on her body, ripping the flimsy fabric of her shirt so I could get to what lay beneath.

Realizing what was happening, I clenched my teeth and forced a deep breath into my lungs. As I slowly let it out, I pushed back against the aggressive magick that encouraged me to follow that line of thinking. All my aggressions were coming to the fore, riled up by Malleus's enchantment. He wanted my mind to be clouded, to be overly ready to fight, so that I'd fling myself at Max without thinking too hard about it. The only problem was that my combat urges were strongly linked to my sexual urges, and I didn't need to be distracted that way right now. Avery was a handsome woman, yes, I freely admitted that. And something about her stood my hair up in a good way on a regular day.

In itself, that was worrisome to me, but not the worst thing ever. With Malleus pushing my already aggressive nature to dangerous levels, though, I couldn't afford to let any feelings I might have for Avery get away from me. That kind of thing can't be undone, and once I got started, I wouldn't stop.

"You all right?" Avery asked, concern threading through her voice.

"Yes," I said, trying to sound like I meant it. I wasn't going to say anything further but found myself talking anyway. "The cuffs are pushing me again, rousing my emotions. He may not be able to track me through them anymore, but they're still doing their job."

She glanced at me, then back at the road. "That must be rough. I mean, I can tell you're really on edge. Ready to fight. That's not normal, right?"

I shook my head. "No, it's not. Not at all. I mean, I'm *always* ready for a fight. It's my job to be prepared and alert. But this is different. I'm..." It took me a moment to put the words together. "I don't use anger when I fight. It doesn't help me. Anger is a dangerous fuel, and mistakes are made. No, I'm usually in a place of calm and quiet in my mind, even though I may be ripping and tearing at a dozen demons. I need to be clear to be effective." I glanced over at her. "Does that make sense to you at all?"

She nodded the whole time I spoke. "Oh, of course."

"Really?"

Avery smiled without taking her eyes off the road. I was glad she did that because having her smile at me just then would have been hard to take. I kept my mouth shut and listened.

"I may not have been a demon killer all my life like you, but I've been in training for years. I started late—I never trained in anything until I started at the police academy, but I was surprised to find I liked it." She grinned and shook her head. "I was always the smallest in the group, and the guys had a habit of trying to show me how tough they were. Nothing came easy, you know?"

I didn't know. My earliest memories involved ripping off a goblin's head as a toddler. I'd been born this way, able to defend myself with deadly skill from the start. Even so, I just nodded. I didn't want her to stop talking.

"I learned some solid moves in the academy, but I needed something more against those big guys, so I trained outside of work. I did a little of everything, Krav Maga at one place, Judo at another, even some stick fighting. I eventually found one teacher who helped me put it all together. She was even smaller than me, and she knew what I was up against. She talked about what she called 'the stillness within the motion.' Like the eye of a hurricane. I liked that. It made sense to me. The more I emptied my mind when I fought, the better my reactions became. I had to drill constantly to improve my skills, but when I got out of my own head, the techniques just jumped right out. Whenever some big guy was outmuscling me and I got mad enough to put everything I had into beating him, I only wore myself out and lost anyway. If I stayed calm, stayed in my stillness, I'd usually find a way to win." She laughed and shook her head. "Sorry, I'm babbling."

I realized that listening to her calmed me. Although the constant buzzing of Malleus's cuffs still pulsed within me, I could breathe again. My own stillness had returned. *She understands me.* I saw her glancing my way, waiting for my response.

"You do talk a lot." The side-eye she gave me nearly prompted me to laugh. "But yes, that's exactly it. That stillness. I can hold it together, but Malleus is messing with my stillness in a huge way."

Avery frowned. "We'll just have to take it out of his hide, then." She glanced at her phone, then back out into the night, getting her bearings. "The address is around the corner up there east of us. We can park up here on Heights next to Marmion Park. No one should bother the Jeep and we can get to it pretty quickly if need be."

She pulled the car off the main road and settled us into a parking spot. The entire corner of the block was a city park with trees, grass, and picnic tables, and at that time of evening, we were alone.

We got out and Avery checked her gun and ammunition. She grimaced as she counted rounds. She'd used quite a few on the demon back at Cyrus's place.

"Ariana's got more in the back," I suggested. "I'm sure she wouldn't mind if you borrowed a few."

Avery's eyebrows rose. "Oh? Show me."

I opened the rear hatches of the Jeep and moved the boxes of gear out of the way, then pushed a button as I'd seen Ariana do. A thick section of the floor lifted out of place and tilted towards us until it was completely vertical, where it locked with a click. I unlatched the panel that faced us and slid it aside to reveal several guns nestled in custom foam insets along with magazines, all loaded. Other items were neatly organized and labeled. There might have been a grenade. Or three.

"Holy. Shit." Avery appeared impressed. "I'm pretty sure most of this is illegal."

I shrugged. "It is Texas, though. That's what Ariana says. And she says she has a license for most of it."

"Most of it?"

I shrugged again. "Some of it's enchanted. Hard to license that."

Avery shook her head and ran her fingers over a few of the handguns displayed. She found one that was twin to the one she carried and appropriated three of the loaded magazines next to it. She started to put them in her pockets, then froze as I pointed to another small chest.

"You'll want something from in there, I think."

She opened the box and pulled out a heavy padded belt with attachments strategically located.

"Oh yeah, now we're talking!" She adjusted it, changed a few of the attachments, and clipped it around her waist. It settled rather fetchingly on her hips. Her hands were an efficient blur as she loaded the belt with gear and snapped her sidearm into the holster. I thought she was finished, but a wide grin appeared on her face and she reached out and touched a slightly larger weapon that had a curved magazine beneath it. I recalled Ariana appropriating it from a security goon back when we'd stormed Elias Bress's building. "I do love a short-barrelled AR," Avery murmured, but then she shook her head and left the weapon there as she let her fingers drift down to rest on what looked like a stubby shotgun. She smiled even wider and shook her head. "Ariana, you clever girl." She pulled the weapon from its resting place and examined it briefly before grabbing some shells from a nearby box and sliding them inside.

"What do you mean?" I didn't pay much attention to guns. They were effective, yes, but I'd been killing people easily enough with my own natural weapons for centuries, so although I recognized some of their differences, I was far from knowledgeable.

Avery didn't take her eyes from her task, and she kept loading shells into the gun until it was full. "Sawed-off shotguns are very much against the law. This is a Mossberg Shockwave. It's short as hell, but because they made it a certain way, it's classified a little differently. Totally legal, and exactly what I want right now."

"Why not take the other one?" I asked as she closed up the Jeep.

"Because the other houses are too close," she answered. "A bullet from that, or even my Glock, could easily go right through a wall and hit someone in the next house over. Not as much chance of that with this thing. I usually don't have a choice, but with all of Ariana's toys, I do."

I shook my head and almost snorted at her caution, but I realized she was right. I knew that some bullets were bigger, some smaller, and some more powerful than others. I couldn't have told you which was which, but I knew Avery knew, and as much as I generally didn't give a crap about other humans, I'd not want an innocent harmed on our account either. Protecting innocents was actually my job. I just had a rough way of doing it.

"Right. Ok, let's move. I'll veil us until we get in. Stay close to me."

"You know which one it is?" Avery asked, surprised.

I looked down the street. A block away, I noticed the play of energies above the trees, the same sickly green power that we'd seen back at Cyrus's place. To my Fae sight, it may as well have been a bonfire.

"Yeah. Follow me."

I wish I could tell you that having Avery a few inches away from me was a pleasant situation, but that would be a lie. My body was already on high alert, and I was twitchy, high-strung, and ready to either fight or do other things. I could smell the perfume she favored, a delicate floral scent that had far more of my attention that it should have. My heightened senses could feel the heat of her, the nearness of her, and the fact that she was a fighter and heavily armed only made her more attractive to me. To be honest, she could have worn a potato sack and I'd still have been interested. I tried to put it all out of my mind as we jogged on the sidewalk towards the house.

We paused when we reached the corner and gave Malleus's place a good look. The house was well over a hundred years old, a white, gabled Victorian place that even boasted a small tower on one corner. Tall trees surrounded a good-sized corner lot on three sides, protecting the house in the middle. White paint chipped and flaked from the walls in several places, and the yard was overgrown, the bushes shaggy and unkempt. Even so, the house still stood proudly intact, lending the impression that it was once a cozy, well-loved home. A wraparound porch surrounded the main floor, elevated from the ground by a short brick wall. I'd seen those out here before. It meant there was a sunken basement of sorts beneath the first floor, unusual here in Houston, but more common in the late 1800's. *We'll go in down there*, I thought. *His conjuring circle is probably there anyway.*

The corner we faced had a few shrubs and a waist high iron fence that looked decorative rather than useful for keeping anyone out. Anyone could hop it. However, this fence glowed with a tracery of power that stretched into a dome over the entire house. Of course, he'd warded it. Any sorcerer would, but that wouldn't keep me out. My usual plan would be to bully my way through it, Faerie thug that I am, leading to two possibilities. One: I alerted Malleus, thus negating the advantage of surprise Ariana suffered to provide. Two: the effort might leave me exhausted and vulnerable, and an attempt to the same might kill Avery if she tried it. She was strong, but there was a lot about her power we didn't know, and it certainly wasn't worth taking a risk in trying to find out if she could survive that effort like I could.

"That fence is warded," Avery whispered, surprising me. Her ability to sense magick was improving.

"It is," I agreed. "I can get through it myself, but it'll be ugly. I'll have to hit it fast and hard and I don't know if I can bring you along with me."

"I. . ." Avery hesitated, then pushed ahead, "I think I can get us both through quietly."

I turned to face her. "I don't mean to be rude, but really?" I hadn't been privy to Avery's training curriculum, but I didn't think Ariana had taught her enough to do something like that yet.

"We were working on wards last week," she explained as she scanned the fence, her pretty eyes narrowed in concentration. "That ward feels really strong, but Ariana's are beefier than that one. I got through one of hers last time, and she was pretty excited about it. Said she couldn't even feel it. She showed me how to be sneaky." She frowned. "I don't have the stuff I need to do it, though. I don't carry those herbs with me like she does."

"You don't really need them," I offered. "That kind of spellwork is more about the intent and focus of the caster. The herbs she uses serve as props that get her in the right frame of mind to do the work, but they're not totally necessary."

"Really? Well, why don't you do it?"

I blinked at her as I tried to come up with a short answer. "It's something I was born with. I'm naturally able to get through most wards," I said, leaving out the part about how much it hurt when I did that. "I haven't needed to practice slipping inside one quietly because I'm good at getting through them the other way. For centuries, it didn't even matter if they knew I was coming, I'd bust my way in, catch the bad guy, and handle him. This is different. A ward this strong might incapacitate me as well as alert him. It's important that we get in quietly, and you have the knowledge to make that happen. Trust it." She frowned, doubt showing on her face. "If you've done this with Ariana, you can do this here, herbs or no herbs. But you have to believe you can do it, and your focus has to be spot on." I watched her think it over, then added, "Or we could just lob a couple of those grenades in there. That would be fun, right?"

She laughed softly. I thought she might have considered it, just for a second or two. I liked that about her. Then she shook her head. "Nah. Firstly, explosions would have police here in minutes. Secondly, they could be dangerous to folks who live next door. Oh, and there's also a chance they'd just bounce off the ward and back into our laps."

I nodded. "Reasonable concerns. It's your show, then. Where do you want to go in?"

She surveyed the yard and pointed to a spot off to one side, right next to the trees that bordered the lot. "There. From that spot, we'll have some cover from those bushes all the way up to the house."

I looked where she indicated and saw the warded fence curving into the yard until it intersected the bordering trees. The resulting corner was shielded from most of the light coming in from the streetlamps and there was, indeed, cover all the way to the house beyond the fence.

"Good choice," I said. Steeling myself against the nearness of her, I muttered, "Stay beside me. Let's move."

There was no traffic to speak of at the late hour, so we made a beeline for the shadowed corner of the yard and knelt there together. That close, I could feel the ward's power making the hairs on my arms stand up. I revised my earlier assessment: If I pushed through it, I'd be battered senseless. Next to me, Avery had her hands open as if she had them pressed against a window a few inches from the surface of the ward. If she'd gotten through Ariana's shield even once, then she had a better than average chance of getting through this one. Her inexperience and lack of preparation were worrisome, but Ariana had said she was a quick study, and her strength in magick was prodigious, if unschooled. A good chance was far better than none at all, and we didn't have time or other options at our disposal, so I waited and hoped.

She turned to look at me and whispered, "You said I don't need the stuff, right? It's just to help me get in the right frame of mind?"

"Exactly."

Her mouth tightened as she considered this. She nodded once. "All right, I'm on it." She turned back to the warded fence and closed her eyes. Silent moments passed as she gathered her thoughts and calmed her mind, purging herself of the doubt that often plagued her. When she'd found the stillness in her mind that she needed, she began to whisper the chant Ariana had taught her. With her right hand, she reached off to one side and gathered a pinch of thin air. This she appeared to deposit into her upturned left palm. The chant continued, and she repeated the motion twice more. I smiled as I realized what she was doing. She was visualizing the herbs needed for the spell, creating them in her mind as clearly as if she was touching them. If you imagine something hard enough, your body doesn't know the difference between what's imagined and what's real, and she'd figured that out.

Clever, I thought.

Avery mashed her palms together and rubbed them briskly, shifting her song into the plea and command it needed to be, urging the ward to open itself to us. Her power flared inside her, clear to my Fae senses, startling me with its intensity. *Wow, girl's got game,* I thought. She definitely had some Fae in her bloodline. That would have to be explored at some point. I stopped myself before I began thinking about exploring other things and focused on her spellwork.

Avery moved her hands in a slow circular motion as she manipulated the power of the ward. She clasped her opened hands together like a diver and drove them directly into the energy field. They penetrated easily, and I felt no answering surge from the ward. It stayed quiet. Avery turned her palms outward and eased her hands apart as though drawing a pair of huge curtains open. She kept chanting but surprised me by releasing her hold on the ward and simply walking through it as though through a normal-sized door. She stepped over the short iron fence, still uttering the spell, and beckoned me through. I ducked my head a little, but I needn't have worried. I felt the edge of the ward at least a foot above me. Once I hopped the fence, Avery slowed her chant and faced the ward again. She brought her hands back to together, and relaxed as the ward closed up behind us, seamless and undisturbed.

"Whew," she breathed, winded. "That was easier than Ariana's, at least, even without the stuff. Whatcha think?"

Again, I blinked at her while I picked my words. I wasn't used to giving effusive praise. Ever. As a child, I'd learned to recognize the lack of a beating as a high compliment during my training. But that was a long time ago, and times change.

"That was. . .impressive."

She smiled. "Thanks." She might have blushed, but I'd already looked away. I didn't need to see that right now.

"All right, let's go. Stay close." I kept the veil over us, hoping to obscure our movements from Malleus well enough that we could at least get the jump on him before he knew we were inside. He knew we were coming, I was certain, but since his ward was undisturbed, he might still think we were on our way. We had a chance.

We brushed our way through the tall plants and came out next to the house. The wooden structure of the house sat on a chest-high brick wall, and if Malleus was anywhere, he was probably in the lower level. We needed to tread carefully. I glanced at Avery and she already had the stubby shotgun in her hands, her sea-green eyes narrowed and watchful. Wow, she looked amazing, every inch the warrior witch. I'd always thought she was a handsome woman, but with the bone cuffs enhancing my aggressive emotions, seeing her in action was really turning me on. I struggled against the swell of desire and managed to get myself back under control.

I've got to get these damned cuffs off. I swear, all I can think about is throwing her down and having my way with her. Not cool.

"Asking me first would get you a lot farther, tough guy."

"What?"

She grinned. "Throw me down? I'm not much for caveman talk like that, but ask me again sometime, and do it nicely. I might consider it."

I squeezed my eyes shut and counted to ten. I don't get embarrassed. I don't. I'm a Fae assassin. Not. Embarrassed. And how had she heard that? I hadn't sent it to her.

"You're thinking pretty loudly, Kane. And I'm hearing better all the time."

Apparently, in focusing on everything else going on, I'd let my mental defenses slip a little. Where a sorcerer like Malleus was concerned, that was a horrendously bad thing. Frustrated, I slammed the walls in my mind down hard enough that I saw her flinch. I glared at her and jabbed my index finger in her direction, struggling to keep my movements precisely controlled. Anger seeped into the words I growled at her.

"Stay. Out. Of my head. If you dig any deeper, what you'll find will keep you awake at night for the rest of your life. Got that?"

Surprise and genuine fear flitted across her face before she mastered it, finishing up with anger. She dealt with that, too, and her features settled into a stern mask that revealed nothing more than cold, hard determination. "Fine. Whatever. Let's get in there and get this done." She turned her back to me and looked ahead.

Satisfied, but not at all happy, I surveyed our surroundings. Our right shoulders were against the wall, and I could see a swimming pool with a small deck up ahead. There were evenly spaced windows in the wall, but they were solid glass and shuttered from the inside. The brick wall ended near the deck, giving way to a wood and screen enclosure that surrounded a huge area behind the house. Its peak rose two stories from the ground, and the whole thing resembled a greenhouse but could have been anything. A door led into the enclosed area, looking like the perfect way in. I let my eyes wander upwards, noting that the lights were off throughout the house. That wouldn't be a problem for me, but it might for Avery. Hmmm. I spotted an open window on the third floor and decided on a plan.

"You go in that door over there as quietly as you can. If you find him, try not to let him see you. Just wait for me. Do you have any defensive spells?"

She shook her head. "No, we've talked about making shields, but haven't practiced yet."

"What about veils?"

"Nope. Still not good at those."

"Is there anything you *are* good at?"

She paused and angrily turned to face me. "I'm good at shooting assholes in the face. Wanna see?"

Oh, damn. My kind of girl. When this is over, we're gonna have to talk.

I nodded, not showing how much I approved of her toughness. "That'll help, yes. But aim for his leg or something. If he's dead, he can't remove the enchantment on these damned cuffs."

She huffed a sigh, disappointed that I didn't rise to the bait, but then shifted back to business mode. "Got it. Shoot to wound if it comes to that. We're looking to capture and secure the guy for interrogation, then?"

"Yep. Just watch yourself, his skills are pretty stout." I looked up at the walls again. "I'm going in through that window up there," I pointed. "You work your way up and we'll meet in the middle."

"Fine. See you inside." She turned away from me and began to stalk along the wall towards the screen door.

She crouched a little as she made her way toward the door, and I followed her with my eyes. I took a moment to admire her ass as she moved, all curves and strength and softness. Before I could catch myself, she froze in her tracks. She slowly turned to look at me over her shoulder and pointedly raised an eyebrow. The tiniest hint of a smile touched the corner of her mouth, then vanished before I was certain I'd seen it at all. Then she dismissed me from her attention and returned to her task. I reached up and dug my claws into the wood above me. I might have some things to look forward to when this was all over. Maybe. But I couldn't take the time to think about that kind of thing right now. It was nothing more than a distraction, at best. I grinned in spite of myself. *As distractions go, that's a good one.* Then shut those thoughts away, pulled myself up onto the wall, and started making like a spider as I headed towards the third-floor window.

I cast a minor glamour over myself to keep the sounds of my claws digging into the old wood from traveling too far. This close to his lair (I still always thought of a sorcerer's home as his lair, old-fashioned as it might be), I didn't think he'd see me if he hadn't already, but scrabbling noises on the walls tended to draw attention. Thus muted, I worked my way up, skirting the lower windows as I climbed. Peeks inside revealed nothing but empty rooms with bare wood floors, a few boxes here and there.

I crawled up directly beneath the window I'd targeted on the third floor. The lights were still out, but I knew I'd see well enough. Clinging to the boards on either side of the window, I reached inside with my senses, searching for any signs of danger. I got nothing. Felt like an empty room to me. *Perfect,* I thought as I slowly raised my head above the level of the sill so I could see inside.

I found myself staring at a very widely spaced pair of bright yellow eyes. They didn't look happy, not at all. A huge, hairy hand shot out of the open window and grabbed a great fistful of my hair. My brain managed one complete thought as I crashed through the window, taking both glass and frame with me.

Well, shit.

Chapter 9

Who the hell does he think he is, talking to me like that? Avery fumed. Anger raced through her, but also a distinct twinge of excitement and she cursed herself inwardly for it. *This is not the time and place for this, geez.* She crept towards the screen door and stopped at the edge of the brick and wood wall.

Christ, he can be such a complete jackass. The smile crept onto her face before she could stop it. *But an* interesting *jackass. Wow.* His human disguise was supposed to be nondescript, boring, and unmemorable. Just a thirty or forty-ish guy like a thousand of them, not remarkable at all. But she could sense him beneath the illusion. His power buzzed constantly, subtly, and only she seemed to notice. Even if he were under a veil, she still detected his presence, which shouldn't have been possible. When he became upset, the intensity of his emotions gave her goosebumps she'd gone to great lengths to hide.

Get a grip, Avy. He's not even human! The instant the thought crossed her mind, she knew it didn't matter a bit to her. She'd seen the Faerie creature beneath the glamour, both in the cave in New Mexico and at Ariana's when the bone manacles had stolen his disguise. She remembered the way his lean muscles bunched and moved beneath his dark skin, a blue so deep it was almost black. She recalled the shining silvery orbs that were his eyes, and the sharp fangs that his full lips revealed whenever they parted. His face, for all its strangeness, was ruggedly handsome, and his features fascinated her. When he moved, it was with supernatural grace and speed, displaying a coordination of mind and body that awed her. When she thought of the way he threw himself at the huge, deadly creature Tanya changed into back in the cave in New Mexico, the memory struck a chord deep within that rang all the way through her bones and out again. *Not human at all.* She sighed. *But still hot as hell. Dammit.*

Leaning carefully around to peek through the screen, she saw a shadowy enclosure that seemed to cover the entire back yard. Wooden support beams held up a corrugated plastic roof, and gravel had replaced the usual grass. Inside, a sidewalk led from the nearby door around to the back of the house, and although difficult to see in the dark and through the screen, Avery felt confident that no one was waiting in the shadows for her. Moving with cool efficiency, she crossed the distance and opened the door to the enclosure, slipped inside, and shut it behind her. Still, nothing moved.

A muffled crash somewhere on the top floor in the house caught her attention, along with the sound of broken glass and heavy impacts. The muted growl of some huge beast reached her, and more thumping.

Kane must have run into something up there! Her heart hammered against her rib cage in fear for him, but with some effort, she shook it off. She reminded herself that Kane was a tough bastard, and he'd probably be fine. Whether he was or not, she needed to stay alert. She checked the safety on the short shotgun she held and slowed her breathing. *Stay focused,* she admonished herself. *Clear the back yard, get inside. Clear each room, then move up a floor. You've done it a hundred times, Avy. You've got this, now get to it!*

Holding the shotgun ready in front of her, Avery followed the sidewalk around to the back of the house. Her surroundings resolved themselves as her eyes adjusted and she saw several potted plants hanging from the rafters and ceiling. Otherwise, the enclosure was empty. As she rounded the corner, she saw that the wraparound porch they had seen in front ended in a balcony in the back of the house. It too, was empty. Beneath it, she could see a workroom with a table attached to one brick wall, empty shelves, and a door that probably led into the basement proper. A thin sliver of light shone from beneath the door.

She darted to the wall next to the door, turned the knob, and pulled the door wide open before flattening herself against the bricks again. A golden glow came from the empty space beyond the door, but all remained silent. Another crash from upstairs, followed by a muffled roar of pain, goaded Avery into action. She peered around the corner and saw no one waiting there to club her to death. She adjusted her grip on the shotgun and crept through the doorway, into the light.

The floor was concrete, and her light footsteps echoed from the bricks no matter how softly she placed her feet. The room she entered was bare, evenly spaced brick columns holding up the house above. Strings of pale yellow Christmas lights lined a few of the rafters and round work-lights were clamped at odd places in the ceiling, providing patchy illumination throughout. Avery caught sight of the room's occupants off to her left, and she whirled in that direction, training the barrel of her gun on them.

A tall, lean man sat in a chair that faced away from Avery, and recognition flooded her as she put a name to the balding, frizzy-headed stranger: Carl, the blind courier. He sat facing a prone figure that sprawled on the floor not far from his feet. A black cloak covered the silent body. *Could be Malleus,* Avery thought. *But what happened here?*

"Carl!" Avery hissed. "Carl, stand up and show me your hands! It's Detective Avery Lynne, and I've got a gun on you right now. Stand up!"

When she received no reply, Avery crept forward, keeping a watchful eye on both suspects. As she approached, she saw that Malleus was inside a casting circle not unlike the ones she'd seen at Ariana's and Cyrus's places. One arm lay across the outer circle, so she knew it wasn't live. The prickle of ill magick touched her, but she noted that it was faint, as though whatever happened was over and done with and the power was fading.

"Carl!" she repeated, louder. "Carl, on your feet right now! Police officer!"

He didn't stand up, but his head slowly swiveled towards her. He looked over his shoulder in her direction, and she saw he still wore his dark glasses. His head swiveled farther. Bones cracked in his neck as his face continued turning until it was staring at her from straight over his backbone. His expression didn't change at all.

Oh, she thought, *oh that's got trouble written all over it.* She made sure the safety was off on the shotgun.

"Carl?" She kept her voice even and authoritative. "I'm here to help. Are you all right?"

Carl declined to answer. Instead, he rose to his feet, tottering a little as he caught his balance, then moved unsteadily around the chair. As he turned, his body came in line with his head, and gruesome popping noises accompanied the adjustment. His head tipped a little to one side and hung at an angle as though its supports were uncertain.

"On the floor, right now! Hands behind your head!" Avery knew that there wasn't a hope in hell of his compliance but found security in following procedure. As she feared, Carl ignored her commands and took a halting step forward, looking somewhat like a marionette with a couple of broken strings. "Don't make me hurt you, Carl!"

Carl took another step. His shaking hands rose towards his chest, where he grasped the fabric of his ratty t-shirt. It tore away, exposing the pale white skin beneath. His chest was narrow and emaciated, and Avery made out the outlines of his ribs. She also noticed that something moved inside Carl's abdomen. Beneath the skin of his stomach, it squirmed and roiled, struggling to emerge.

Before Avery uttered another word, Carl's thin body split from collarbone to waist. The gruesome crack widened as bloody fingers pushed their way out from inside to grasp the ragged edges of the wound. Sharp, bony claws glistened wetly at the end of ghastly fingertips, and they pried the gap open. The dim light revealed a bloody, inhuman face inside Carl's body, a nightmarish grin of fangs below a pair of gleaming yellow eyes. The demon struggled to work its way out, but the opening wasn't wide enough. Yet.

"Nope," Avery muttered, "I'm not having any of that today, no sir."

She opened fire with the shotgun, pumped another round, and fired again, the noise of the two shots deafening in the enclosed basement. Even as she pulled the trigger, the creature inside Carl raised one hand and uttered a word in a foul, slithering language that made her skin crawl. A yellowish haze appeared in front of its gesturing hand, flaring brightly as the pellets from the shotgun blasts struck, then ricocheted into the walls on either side.

"Shit!" Avery's eyes went wide as the creature gurgled laughter and continued to work its way out of the opening it had created in Carl's body. Fear coursed through her, and her knees wobbled, their support uncertain. That unsteadiness galvanized her, angered her, and disappeared as her magick boiled up from deep within to give her strength. Her mouth clamped into a thin line as she worked the action of the shotgun, chambering another round and firing again. The shot forced the creature to stop climbing out of Carl long enough to shield itself again with an annoyed wave and another brief flash of energy. It howled in anger before resuming its struggle to heave itself out from the gory hole in the homeless man's torso. Seeing it distracted, Avery took a determined step forward, chambering another round and firing the fourth shot at the hideous thing from only a few feet away.

She'd timed the shot well and was rewarded by a yowling screech of agony as some of the pellets got through, striking both Carl and the demon he carried. Carl's body jerked to his right and tumbled to the floor facedown, trapping the creature inside his torso. One hideous arm reached out from underneath, trying to gain purchase on the wood floor. The body spasmed and flopped as the demon within struggled to find its way out. Grimacing, Avery stepped up and put a foot on Carl's back, pinning the body down.

"Sorry, Carl," Avery snapped. She pointed the barrel at the small of his back, right where she knew the thing's head had been. Her magick found its way into her arms, and her body glowed with a faint blue light as she channeled her power down into her hands, and into the firearm she trained on the dead man below her. The shot blew his back wide open, and a shrill wail of protest reached her, sounding farther and farther away as seconds ticked by. Puffs of black flame appeared, removing a few stray bits of demon, and all fell silent as they vanished.

She reached up with one shaking forearm and wiped something drippy from her forehead as she looked down at the body. Whatever had been inside Carl was long gone. And Carl was a mess. The faint odor of rotting flesh reached her, and she realized that Carl had been dead since not long after they'd last seen him. *Malleus killed him,* she thought, and she turned angry eyes toward the silent, prone figure that lay nearby.

Turning the shotgun belly-up, she deftly snatched four fresh shells from the carrier on her belt with one hand, slid them into the shotgun in two swift motions, then chambered another round and trained the weapon on the downed figure.

"All right, Malleus. No sudden moves. Get on your knees and put your hands behind your head. I'll happily help you up if I have to, but you won't like how I do it. I said on your knees, asshole."

The body remained silent and unmoving.

Avery frowned. She decided to check him over from a distance, rather than move close enough for him to spring a trap. Ignoring Carl's stench, she took as deep a breath as she could manage and released it. *Gotta calm down. Gotta focus.* Remembering the lessons Ariana had taught her, she reached out with her feelings, probing the body with her magick. A sense of quiet surrounded the body, though not the same kind of harsh silence that existed when a mind was shielded. *Like Kane's,* she thought, remembering how his mental walls had come down earlier, and she winced at the memory. She'd not meant to upset him. Indeed, she had hoped that being flirty would. . .would what? She admitted to herself that she had no idea what she'd been doing but banished that line of thinking and refocused on the body. She became aware of its steady, slow breathing, and unhurried heartbeat. Still, nothing moved.

"Malleus," Avery warned, her voice low and dangerous, "In case you missed all the noise, I've got a shotgun. I don't like you. Don't give me a reason to express my feelings further. Stay still or you'll end up like Carl over there."

Avery darted forward and grabbed the figure's left hand with hers, skillfully applying what she knew was a painful wristlock. She carefully laid the shotgun on the floor within easy reach before adding her other hand to apply more pressure. Her knee pressed diagonally across the body's shoulder and back, pinning it down as she pulled the left arm up into a hammerlock. In moments, she had the body cuffed, searched, and rolled over onto his back. Up close she saw that he wore black jeans and an expensive button-down shirt, also black. The black hood still half-covered his face.

"Let's see what we've got here." Avery retrieved her shotgun before carefully pulling the cloth hood away.

The cowl fell aside to reveal a man of middle years, with dark hair and a stubble of unshaven beard shadowing a square jaw. His nose had been broken at some point and healed not quite well enough to hide the fact. Deep-set eyes remained closed beneath bushy black eyebrows. A thin scar ran down one side of his cheek. Although unconsciousness left him slack and inert, he looked every inch a villain.

Is he though? The strength of that thought surprised her. It seemed to explode out of her subconscious as if screaming at her. She shook her head and took a closer look at the silent figure.

He was tall, nearly six feet, and leanly muscled. Something caught her eye and she carefully reached over to pull open the collar of his shirt, undoing the first couple of buttons as she did so.

At first, she thought they were tattoos, intricate designs that snaked their way across his chest. Closer inspection revealed that they weren't simple ink, but scars instead, aggressive, dark designs that whispered faint promises of power.

"Oh, come on, that's a sorcerer if I ever saw one!" she blurted.

And yet, the feeling persisted.

Before she could explore it any further, an enormous impact shook the house above her. She hunched her shoulders and brought up the shotgun as she searched for the source of the noise. Heavy footsteps slammed into the wood overhead, followed by a bestial roar that was cut off with several loud grunts. Another crash, a moment of silence—and then an enormous figure exploded into the basement, flying down a short stairwell and landing in a shower of wood and sheetrock from the doorway.

Avery swiveled towards the creature as it tried to rise, but then it sighed and fell flat on its face. It was a huge, blocky thing, humanoid, but with far too many muscles to be human. It reminded her of the old version of the Incredible Hulk, back when it was gray and hadn't yet taken on his trademark greenness. *God, I'm a such a geek to know that,* she thought, never taking her eyes off the beast.

It sighed again, settling into death. Moments later, silent black flames erupted from the demon's skin, dissolving it and sending it back whence it came.

"Sorry that took so long."

The sound of Kane's voice made her heart leap, but she quelled her excitement. She spotted him as he made his way down the stairs, and her heart thumped harder as she saw that he wasn't wearing the glamour to hide his true appearance. His blue-black skin glistened in the yellow light, powerful muscles on full display as he stalked into view. He moved with such grace and fluidity, she couldn't get enough of the sight of him. When he turned his silvery eyes towards her, it was all she could do to keep up her own disguise, that of stone-cold Detective Avery Lynne, impervious to anyone's charms. But she was definitely pervious.

Damn, she thought, *I've got it bad. Yep.* Gritting her teeth, she shut out those thoughts and got down to business.

Chapter 10

Throwing the demon through the cellar door had been unnecessary, but fun. I was a little disappointed to see the black flames come for it because that meant the fight was over. It had been a sturdy creature, little more than dumb muscle, but those kinds of brutes are still dangerous, even for me. We'd trashed the two floors above us as we'd fought, but I had to admit that the furious tussle had done me some good. It had helped abate the nervous, angry energy that the cuffs seemed to be pumping through me. And I'd managed a tour of the empty house as we'd bashed our way through it. Not much up there save a few boxes and a bed in one room. Although austere, the place looked well-kept. It was no hobo den, that much was certain.

I followed the demon down the basement stairs at a leisurely pace, taking my time. I heard heavy breathing and recognized Avery's heartbeat right away, strong and excited. She was down there. The thought made me happier than it should have. It took a moment for me to gather up what composure I could find so I wouldn't be weird.

"Sorry that took so long," I said, trying to be reassuring. Her heartbeat kicked up a notch, and I felt a sudden burst of excitement run through her before she squashed it, just as I had my own. I caught sight of her as I descended the stairs, and she couldn't have looked more perfect to me. Her head was tilted back, and her eyes were fastened firmly on me, the shotgun held ready in her hands. Blood-spattered from combat, a crimson smear decorated her forehead. She resembled a warrior woman from centuries past, painted in the blood of her enemies. I liked it. I liked it a lot. I tried to keep that thought from showing on my face as well as smooth my emotions over so she wouldn't sense anything.

"It's fine." she replied, "I think I've got Malleus under control down here, but. . ." she paused as she gathered her thoughts, "but something's definitely wonky about this whole thing." She nodded at the silent figure on the floor, cuffed and unmoving. "I'd be willing to bet that's him, but he doesn't feel right."

I clothed myself in my usual human glamour out of habit and was surprised to see a hint of disappointment flit across her face. I tried to ignore it for the moment. *Something to look into later,* I thought. "Doesn't feel right? How so?" I moved closer and looked down at his face. He seemed about the right height and had the distinctive air of foul magick on him. That kind of power was hard to hide. Its aura clings to the user, making them easier for Grims like me to pick out. His energy had the same foul taint to it that I'd sensed at the playing field, but it had nearly dissipated. *Strange.*

I looked over at the mess nearby, a body nearly blown in half. "Trouble?"

Avery glanced in that direction, blew a stray lock of her black hair out of her face and nodded. "Yeah, that's Carl. Or was, anyway. A demon tried to crawl out of him when I came in. Had to shoot him, but he was already dead. That's some scary stuff."

I had to agree. Using a human corpse as a jumping off point for a demon wasn't easy to do and spoke volumes as to the depth of Malleus's skills, as well as his level of crazy.

"Great job," I said. She tried not to look pleased but failed. I turned back to Malleus and caught sight of the ritual scars that peeked out from beneath his shirt. I ripped the shirt open, sending buttons flying, and took in the arcane designs he'd carved into his own flesh. "Yeah, this has got to be him. Only a sorcerer of his caliber would know what those sigils mean, and only a crazy one would inscribe them on himself. This is him."

I wondered if I should just stomp his face in right then but only sighed. If I did that, I'd most certainly lose my hands. He needed to remove the cuffs himself or the bargain would stand, and he couldn't do that with a bashed-in skull. I decided, for once, that talking might be more effective. *Kane the diplomat, that's me.*

"Grab that chair for me, would you?" Avery complied, bringing the wooden chair closer while I picked up Malleus's limp body. He was breathing, heartbeat steady. *So why is he still unconscious? What happened here?* I planted him in the chair and stepped in front of him. We needed answers, and I knew what I'd have to do to get them. Didn't like it, though. Probing the mind of a sorcerer like Malleus was seldom a safe thing to do. Even so, I've seen his like before, and I knew I would again. This had to be done. "If he does anything threatening at all, blow his head off."

"No!" Avery hissed. "That'll ruin your chance of getting those cuffs off! I can't!"

I turned to glare at her. "Do it. I'm just going to scope him out, step inside his mind. I can't risk anything happening to you. If he tries anything at all, shoot him. I'll be fine." She glared right back at me, her angry eyes matching mine. Sweet mother goddess, she gave me some feels. I tried what I hoped was a reassuring tone, "Look, I've got this." After a few tense seconds, Avery sighed in frustration and nodded once as she brought her shotgun to a ready position.

I faced Malleus. His head lolled to one side as he slept, unmoving and quiet. I moved closer and slowed my breathing until I was calm enough to do the job. My mind needed to be clear for that kind of work, and it took longer than usual to get there. Once I was ready, I closed my eyes and sent my awareness into the sleeping sorcerer.

Nothing. Inside Malleus's head, there was nothing but dark and quiet, a basement with no windows and no lights. It wasn't shielded, it was just...empty. I drifted as I tried to remain calm, tried to relax and feel my way around. I couldn't remember the last time I'd been in such a silent mind. There should have been images, thoughts flying around, feelings washing over me, but all the usual signs of life were simply absent. This felt like an old, empty warehouse. It was awfully unusual. Since Malleus was alive, I knew there had to be *something*. I kept looking.

Somewhere in the distant dark, something caught my attention. It was a faint sense of pressure, nothing more. I turned in that direction and willed myself to move, seeking more of the same. The feeling intensified, and I figured I was on to something. I remained watchful, cautious of the usual tripwires and traps that any sorcerer might leave for an unwary interloper but found none at all. It was damned odd.

A tiny pinprick of light appeared, and I accelerated, speeding my awareness in that direction. The brightness resolved itself into a blob of golden light, shining in an otherwise eternal dark. I slowed my approach and drifted closer. It appeared to be a perfect sphere, swirling with golden light, mixed with flashes of sky blue. I'd seen that particular hue before. I moved closer, coming right up to the surface of the sphere and surrounded it with my magick, sensing, feeling, trying to gain a sense of what was inside. I got it, all right. All at once, I recognized what was held within the sphere, and a wave of emotion rocked me. Shocked, I felt my awareness hurtle backwards, upwards, outwards, until I withdrew from Malleus's mind and slammed back into my body. My eyes flew open in astonishment and anger.

I gasped and reeled awkwardly, stumbling as I struggled to catch my breath. Avery was right there.

"What is it? What did you see?"

It took a moment for me to get myself together as outrage and surprise flowed through me. I forced the words out. "Ariana. Ariana's in there. Her spirit is locked inside him somehow."

Avery's eyes flew wide, "Oh shit! If she's in there, where's Malleus?"

Avery whipped out her phone and dug out Cyrus's business card. She dialed the number and put the phone on speaker mode. I didn't tell her I would have heard it anyway. It rang for a few seconds, and Cyrus answered.

"Bell, Book, and Cauldron...Detective? Is that you?"

"We're fine, just listen! Is Ariana still with you? Is she all right?"

"Oh, yes, she's fine. Still sleeping, but nothing magickal can get to her from the outside. I've got her comfortably situated in my circle, safe as can be." He paused. "Did you find him? Are you two all right?"

"We did, but you need to bind her. Tie Ariana up or something, right away."

There was another pause, then his bewildered reply, "What? Why? She's not going anywhere. . ."

There was a thump and Cyrus grunted before falling silent. The phone clattered as he dropped it to the floor.

"Cyrus! Cyrus, are you there?"

I already knew what was coming, and I wasn't disappointed. No, I wasn't disappointed at all—I was furious. After a brief silence, we heard someone pick up the phone. Malicious feminine laughter tumbled out of the speaker.

"Well, well, I declare, this body is amazing."

100

I took the phone from Avery's hand and she didn't fight me. "Malleus, you bastard."

Ariana's voice carried a thick Southern accent, all slyness and confidence. She responded, "Now, now, there's no need to be rude, Kane. Don't you have a job to do? Tick, tock, my friend. Time grows short."

"Look, asshole, I've got your real body right here. I'd be more than happy to disassemble it for you and give it back to you in a lunchbox."

That laughter again. Hearing Ariana's voice driven by Malleus turned my stomach, but all I could do was fume in anger as I listened.

"Feel free to do as you wish with it. I'm perfectly fine with the body I'm in now. Gracious, I am *gor*-geous! This certainly wasn't part of the plan, but I'm an opportunist at heart. The things I'll do with this body—I can hardly wait to take it for a spin. Oh, I feel I should warn you that whatever you do to my old shell, Ariana will feel it. Even if she can't drive it around, she's in there, feeling every bump and bruise you've given her. She'll live out her days in my old body, while I enjoy hers. And enjoy it, I shall. Mmmm, yes, I certainly will." Her voice became harder, and more of Malleus came out. "Now get to work. This happy accident doesn't alter our deal in the slightest. And the deadline is rapidly approaching. I'll get what I want one way or the other, but I'd just as soon have you do your job!"

The line disconnected. I considered it a minor victory that I didn't fling Avery's phone into the wall, choosing to gently hand it to her in spite of the intense rage flowing through me.

"My job," I growled, struggling to control my anger, "is to rip guys like him into bloody pieces."

"Well, we'll have to figure out how to get him back in his own body, first," Avery warned, not unkindly. This close, I could feel her emotions, and knowing that she was as angry as I was somehow helped. "We've got to find her."

"By the time we get back to Cyrus's place, Malleus will be long gone. He could hide forever in her body if he wants to, even just skip town with it. We'd never find him."

Without warning, Avery gasped and froze, a look of horror appearing on her face.

"What is it?"

She started slowly shaking her head. "I just had an awful thought. The deadline's approaching, right?" I nodded. We had a couple of hours at most. "If someone killed Max before you fulfill your agreement, what happens?"

I blinked at the thought. Then my stomach dropped into my feet as my mind followed that possible course of events, which led to a stark conclusion.

"If someone kills Max before I do, then I'd be unable to keep my part of the bargain. I'll forfeit my hands and my illusory ability. Rules are rules."

She nodded, her sea-green eyes wide. "Max knows to avoid you right now. We all know you don't want to hurt him in the first place, but just in case, he'd stay away from you. But Ariana. . .?"

I growled, "Ariana can get pretty close to Max, and he'd be happy to see her. She could easily slip a silver-edged knife between his ribs before he knows it's not her."

"Which would kill him and maim you."

Beautiful and smart. If I survive this mess, I might just have to figure out how to date a human.

Avery burst into motion, picking up the spent shotgun shells that littered the floor. "We've got to get to Max before she does. He does. Whatever! I'll try to reach him at the hotel from the car, but I thought he was already planning to hole up somewhere else. Damn, I wish I had his cellphone number!"

I hoisted Malleus's limp body over my shoulder. "We'll need a way to switch them back into their own bodies. Any ideas?"

Avery tucked the last shell into a pocket and shook her head. "I'm still wet behind the ears where spellcraft is concerned. Anything I do at this point is luck or instinct, Kane. Other than the wards, I haven't had much time to learn the finer points of this stuff."

I growled, frustrated. "We need Cyrus. Now that we know what happened, he might have the skills to fix this."

"Cyrus may be dead. Malleus might have killed him."

"True, but he might not have. And it's about the only shot we have with so little time left." I did some quick calculations, then continued, "Look, I can get to Max's hotel at least as fast as you can drive me. You need to go get Cyrus and see if he's alive. If he knows what's happened, he can probably find a way to switch them back."

Avery frowned at me. Damn, she looked good when she did that. She looked even better when she smiled, but I figured it might be a while before I'd see that expression on her face again.

"Max has likely moved already."

"I'm a good tracker." I offered, "Part of the job. I can find him. But I can't do that and check on Cyrus, too."

Avery eyed me warily, reluctant to leave. "I don't like it. You'll need me if Malleus is going after Max. Cyrus is in the other direction and might be dead anyway."

"It's the best chance we've got, Avy."

My use of her nickname made something flutter inside her. I felt it. She flashed a smile at me in surprise before resuming her intense expression while I dealt with the damned butterflies cavorting in my stomach. I knew I might die soon, but after seeing that smile, I'd die happy. Then I rolled my eyes at myself. *Damn these cuffs, making me feel things.*

Avery sighed in resignation. "All right. I'll take the body to Cyrus. Wait, what if he wakes up and he's Malleus again?"

"Duct tape," I answered. "It's in the Jeep."

Chapter 11

The wind whipped past me, pulling my hair away from my face beneath my veil. I rode atop a big rig truck as it motored west along the freeway they called 610. The vehicle changed lanes and another rig pulled alongside it on its way to pass. I hopped to the speedier truck and settled there, already looking for another, faster moving vehicle I could leapfrog to. I was capable of running at ridiculously high speeds, but these trucks were faster, and I knew I'd be less tired upon arrival. As it was, it took all my patience to sit still on top of the truck and let it do the work for me.

I knew the road would hook to the south and take me almost directly to the hotel in which we'd met Max. There was no guarantee he'd be there, of course, but that was the logical place to start. One day, I'd have to start carrying a cell phone. *Damned inconvenient,* I thought. *I'll just lose the thing.* Still, they had their uses. If I'd had Max's number programmed in one, I'd have been able to call him right then and there, but since I didn't, I had to go to him. *I hope he's there,* I thought. No matter where he was, all it would take would be for Malleus/Ariana to call him and set up a meeting elsewhere and I'd be hard-pressed to find them. My tracking skills were top notch, part of the GrimFaerie skillset, but time was running out, and I doubted I could find him before the clock struck and my hands were severed from my wrists. *No pressure.*

As I peered into the night, looking for my next target, a knowing came over me. A vision. I closed my eyes and saw Max in a hotel room, though not the same one we'd seen. He pecked away at his laptop while Edge lounged in a chair, reading a book. Two enormous goons I hadn't seen before stood on either side of the hotel room door, looking solid and imposing. One carried an impressive assault rifle, but the other held an odd-looking weapon. The back half of it looked like an ordinary bolt-action rifle, but it had a vertical foregrip and a peculiar attachment on the business end, a clunky pyramid of some kind, its base facing outward where the barrel should have been.

Max's phone chirped, and he thumbed it awake to find a text from Ariana, a request for the address of the hotel and the room number. She had news but wanted to share it with him in person. Without hesitation, he texted a response. The phone screen loomed larger in my mind's eye and I noted the information. His new hotel was in the same part of town as our previous meeting place, but a few streets over. I knew right where it was. The vision faded, and I smiled.

"Thank you, Mother," I whispered as I opened my eyes. I got no reply from the Goddess, but I knew she heard me. She always did. She wasn't often so forthcoming with assistance, but when she was, I gratefully took it.

Too many minutes later, a green sign next to the freeway warned me that my exit was coming up. I scanned the vehicles closest to my ride and picked a route that would not only be fun but would take me right to the shoulder. I leapt from the top of the eighteen-wheeler, keeping my veil in place. The driver of the maroon suburban might have seen a disturbance in their line of sight, a formless blur in the air, but didn't pay any attention until I landed on the hood of their car, denting the metal. The vehicle swerved, so I hopped onto a passing pickup, bounced from there onto an armored car, and finally tapped the roof of a Volkswagen on my way over. When I landed on the shoulder of the road, I left a lot of screeching and honking behind me, but a glance told me that I hadn't caused more than confusion and a couple of close scrapes. The cars kept moving, and the commotion disappeared into the night.

I hopped the concrete barrier, fell into the empty darkness beyond and landed with a thump in a grassy area alongside the overpass. The moment I touched down, I ran for all I was worth, following my senses and keeping an eye out for street signs as I raced towards the hotel—and the werewolf king.

The tower of brick, steel, and glass rose up into the night, brightly lit against the dark. I thought about taking the stairs, but my intuition screamed at me, as it often does. *Fine,* I thought, *I like climbing better anyway.* I ran around the perimeter of the building until I faced the side that I thought Max's window faced. For the second time that night, I dug my claws into a wall and began working my way up to the top.

Halfway up, I reached out with my magick, questing for Max. He had a profoundly strong aura, and I'd become acquainted with it of late. It didn't take long for me to find it, and I angled my ascent in that direction.

The hotel was not quite as tall as the previous one, and its concrete spiral parking garage was right below and behind me. Max was on the top floor of the place, as expected. I clawed my way towards the window nearest to where I sensed the king's presence, and positioned myself alongside it so I could peer in. Fortunately, the blinds were open, and I was afforded a clear view of the room's interior.

Max sat at his desk pretty much as I'd seen him in my vision, resting his bearded chin on one huge fist while the other hand manipulated the mouse next to his laptop. His eyes darted back and forth as he scanned whatever data he found there. I turned my head a bit and saw that Edge was no longer present, but the book he'd been reading was lying face down on the chair he'd vacated. The two goons stood guard by the door.

I was just about to rap on the window to get Max's attention, but someone beat me to it, knocking loudly on the door to the suite. One of the goons looked through the peephole and I heard him announce Ariana's name. Max nodded with a smile and rose from behind the desk as the goon opened the door.

Ariana sauntered in, a sly smile on her face. She tossed a coy glance at the guard as she walked past him, though he ignored it. She was walking with far more hip sway than I'd ever seen her use, and her eyes sparkled with eagerness. She didn't say a word as Max circled around his desk, arms open as he went to meet her. He didn't see the knife in her belt, but I could. I recognized it from Cyrus's place. Prominently displayed. Expensive. Silver alloy. Max wrapped his long arms around her, and she returned his hug before letting go with her right hand. As I watched, she eased it towards the knife.

Hotel windows are really thick, but I was pretty pissed off. I reared back and punched it, throwing as much frustration into the blow as I could. It shattered inward in a cascade of deadly shards. I launched myself inside, bounded across the room, and tackled Ariana and Max to the floor. *Oof, he's built like a truck!* Ariana's dagger fell from her fingers, and I left it where it landed, content for the moment it was out of her reach. Furious, Ariana turned over, pointed at Max and spoke a couple of sharp, arcane syllables before I could get to her. Laying hold of her ankles, I swiveled and flung Ariana's body away from Max. She hit both guards as they surged forward, weapons coming up to fire, and she took them both down in a wild tumble of arms and legs. I heard a thunk as her head smacked into something, and she went limp. *Good,* I thought. *That'll give me time to work this out.*

"Max!" I yelled as I turned, "That's not Ariana!"

108

Unfortunately, Max didn't hear me. The face inches from mine was not the smooth, debonair businessman I'd come to know. His winning smile had been replaced by a horrifying grin that was a little too wide for his face, his canines lengthened into sharp points. His eyes glowed amber-yellow as they burned into mine, and I saw his jaw press forward, bones popping in the process. A cavernous, echoing growl escaped him, and his voice dropped into an impossibly deep register, letting me know without a doubt that the beast in him was coming out, and there was nothing I could to do stop it. His already huge chest expanded, and rips appeared as his muscles rapidly grew beyond the confines of his suit. Dark hair sprouted as he became the wolfman I'd hoped to never see.

"Max, wait!" I held up my hands in a non-threatening gesture. "I can explain!" Rage from the cuffs flowed through me as my heart pounded with excitement, and I struggled to keep the anger suppressed. I desperately needed a cool head here. It did not escape my notice that even though I was veiled, Max fixed his eyes directly on me. *Uh oh,* I thought, *looks like I can't hide from him. And I think Malleus might have tossed off a spell before I could stop him. Bad. All bad.*

His howl of anger was fierce and hot, and I knew I'd lost the chance to reason with him. Before I could even think of what to do next, Max made that decision for me. My next move was to take a backhanded hit across the face and fly into the couch, knocking it over as I tumbled. I performed this action exceedingly well, though I had little to say about it. Max howled again and advanced, fingernails lengthening to deadly claws and his head almost all wolf.

"Max, I'm telling you, it's not her! It's Malleus in her body!" The words barely came out in the right order, my own rage threatening to jumble them completely. I had to focus.

I got to my feet and grabbed the couch, intending to slam it into the werewolf's head as I tried to buy some time. Max snatched it out of my hands like a child's toy and broke it over his knee before flinging the two halves aside.

I've faced a lot of dangerous creatures over the centuries, most of them bigger than me. Watching Max rip his way out of the last remnants of his suit and finish morphing into the biggest and strongest werewolf on the planet, well, that was damned impressive. And scary. Freed of the last confines of human adornment, he stood there and glared at me, emitting a constant bass growl that made my teeth ache. He'd gained at least a foot in height and over a hundred pounds of muscle during his transformation. His arms and hands were furry, but still human-looking, and his legs were more canine in appearance. Enormous muscles bunched and moved beneath a coat of sleek, black fur, struck here and there with hints of silver. Cloaked in his power, he was beautiful to see, and deadlier than anything I'd faced in a while.

Because of Malleus's cuffs (and my natural inclination) all I wanted to do was fling myself into battle with that beast, ripping, tearing, biting, until only one of us remained alive. Every fiber of my being was on edge, just waiting for me to act on that overwhelming impulse. Max took a swipe at me with a clawed hand and I ducked it, as well as the second one, and I dodged just out of his reach.

There was movement in the corner as one of the guards got back to his feet. He struggled to focus on us, pulling his odd-looking rifle to his shoulder as he searched for a target. Behind him, Ariana lifted her head from the floor, still woozy from the fall.

"Sir! Step back, I'll get him!" the guard called out, trying to train his weapon on what he only saw as a blur in the air.

I knew what to do. Skirting the rage that boiled through me, I reached out with my magick and touched the guard's mind. His gaze focused on a spot in between himself and Max as he saw what I willed him to see: a solid version of myself squaring off against the wolfman. The guard smiled a tight little 'gotcha' smile, sighted the contraption on Max, and pulled the trigger.

The shot boomed in the confines of the hotel room and the net burst out of the guard's weapon to launch itself at Max's wolf form, spreading out as it went. It performed perfectly, entangling Max in an eyeblink, the weights around the edges of the wire net snaring him tightly. From the looks of it, the net was made of heavy-duty steel filament, so I was glad I didn't have to fight my way out of it. Max bellowed in fury and snarled as he struggled to get his arms free, but the net held him fast. I bet it hurt, too.

The guard looked confused until I knocked him out, and he slumped to the floor in a boneless heap alongside his buddy. Ariana had made it to her hands and knees, and she turned a furious glare my way. As she opened her mouth to speak, I hit her with a calculated right cross that sent her back to the floor, unconscious.

"Save it, Mal," I said. "I'm not interested in whatever you've got to say right now, especially not if you're going to toss a spell at me." I snatched a pair of handcuffs from one of the unconscious guards and cuffed Ariana's wrists behind her back, mindful not to hurt her. She'd want this body back when all was said and done, and I didn't want to damage it more than necessary. As an afterthought, I ripped a piece from a guard's shirt and stuffed it in her mouth for good measure.

Once she was secured, I picked her up and slung her over my shoulder. Max had fallen to the floor as he struggled to free himself, and he roared again, angry as hell. I wasn't sure how much of Max was awake behind those wolf eyes, but I hoped it was enough to hear me.

"Max, you need to listen. It's not her. Malleus. . ." I started to explain, but Max heaved and bucked on the floor and I heard some of the cables in the net pop. A couple more strands let go and he made it to his feet, ripping his way out of the wiry tangle.

At that point, I did what any smart GrimFaerie would do in that situation. I jumped out the window with Ariana over my shoulder. Who says weeknights are dull?

Chapter 12

I aimed for the top floor of the parking garage and cushioned our fall by land on the roof of a tiny red car. The windows shattered and the roof crumpled like an aluminum can, but it absorbed enough of the shock to keep Ariana from getting whiplash. As much as I wanted to cause Malleus pain, I couldn't do it while he was in her body. I needed to extract him from there and get Ariana back home in her own head. *I hope Cyrus is alive*. I knew some others who could help, but their prices were often extremely high. Like, 'pay off in centuries or body parts' high. Even so, I knew I'd readily go to them if it came to that. Ariana was my friend, and she was well worth whatever I'd need to pay to make her whole again. In the meantime, my job was to keep her body intact while making sure Malleus didn't use it to cause any trouble. Well, any *more* trouble, as he'd already caused plenty. Oh, and I needed to figure out how to get him to remove my cuffs before they cut off my hands. *Just another easy Wednesday,* I thought, shaking my head. Adjusting Ariana's body on my shoulder, I ducked into the nearest stairwell, hoping that getting out of plain sight might help me evade Max long enough to escape and regroup.

The unearthly roar from above let me know that Max escaped the netting completely and was in hot pursuit. I heard and felt a solid thump somewhere above me that confirmed it—he'd landed on the top floor just as I had. With his werewolf senses, he'd find me soon enough. Evading him while carrying Ariana's body would be difficult, if not impossible, and my mind raced to come up with a better plan.

As I passed the landing for the second floor, I heard the deep rumbling of an engine on the far side of the concrete wall. I stopped, veiled myself and Ariana's body, and opened the steel door that led to that level. Halfway across the parking garage, a black and green vehicle was backing into a spot, moving so slowly I figured the driver was either completely unskilled or being unusually careful. The machine looked brand new, and was an odd-looking contraption, a blend of motorcycle and car that had only one wide tire in the rear and two in the front. I'd seen them before, but not up close.

There's my ride.

Still veiled, I sprinted across the empty spaces and slowed as I approached the vehicle. The driver exited, shut the door, and bent over to adjust his tie and windblown hair in the side mirror. The guy looked to be in his early thirties, old enough to have money to buy such toys and young enough to still want them.

I reached into his mind and inserted a powerful suggestion. When it took hold, I adjusted my veil and stood in full view of him. I held out my open palm and waited.

He caught sight of me and straightened up immediately. "Ah!" he greeted me cheerily, "There you are!" He dropped the keys in my palm, oblivious of Ariana's body draped over my shoulder. "Detailed top to bottom and returned here by morning, yeah?"

"Yes sir, that's our company policy," I replied as calmly as I could. I could hear Max pounding the car to pieces somewhere above us. There was a moment of silence, then a red blur of junk flashed past our floor to crash somewhere down below. An instant later, I heard the door at the top of the stairs get ripped off its hinges. "Oh, and you might want to hurry along, sir. I hear there's a bad element in this area. Muggings, you know."

His eyes widened, "No shit? Who'd have thought...Ok, I'm out." He grabbed a duffle from the passenger seat and started racewalking towards the central elevators while I dumped Ariana's body in the car.

I sat in the driver's seat and buckled her in firmly before doing the same for myself. Couldn't have her limp body fly out during a hairpin turn. The car started up with a firm rumble, sounding ready to lay down some rubber, which was exactly what I needed, if only for a short while. I put it in gear and glanced at the entry door I'd used moments before.

Max bulled through it like it was made of aluminum, taking chunks out of the concrete walls around the frame. His jaws opened wide, revealing rows of dangerously sharp teeth, and his claws dug furrows in the concrete surface beneath him as he propelled himself towards us. He was magnificent. And deadly.

I gunned the engine, and the back wheel spun in place for just long enough to worry me before it bit into the pavement and shot us forward. I yanked on the wheel and managed to point us downhill as we sped down the ramp, doing my best to keep the car from slamming into anything nearby. Fortunately, the garage was empty, but I was more worried about anything slowing us down than leaving damage behind. Sometimes, collateral damage could be fun, but not with a werewolf so close behind. I made the back tire squeal as I whipped us around the turn at the bottom of the lane and came around the other side of the garage. I heard Max howl in frustration as he pursued.

The exit lane gate featured an automated wooden arm that barred the way. We blew through it, leaving it in shards in the street, and I muscled the car into a right turn that made all three tires scream in agony, but they did their job, gripping the road hard. The machine responded instantly when I pressed on the gas, its hot little engine ramping up, excited to be let off the leash. Max burst out of the confines of the garage right behind us, running on all fours, his burning eyes focused on me as though I'd stolen his girlfriend. To be fair, I kind of had. I urged the car to go faster and it pulled away from the pursuing werewolf. I sped through a couple of red lights, being thankful that traffic was light that time of night, but threw a veil over us to minimize our exposure.

I glanced over at Ariana and her eyelids fluttered open. *Damn, Malleus is waking up.* He squeezed her eyes shut and opened them again as he caught his bearings. As he turned to look at me, I hit him with another sharp punch that put him right back out. I grimaced as I thought about having to explain all the bruises and the blackened left eye to Ariana when she got back in her own body. She was not gonna be happy with me, but nothing could be done about it right now.

Behind us, I heard Max howl in rage. I extended my senses and found him galloping along the roadside back there, his powerful lungs heaving from the exertion but nowhere near his limits. He'd have plenty of energy left to tear me apart when he finally got his claws on me. The animal part of him reveled in the chase, the hunt.

I was more concerned that he wasn't hiding himself as he chased me. Anyone watching from the surrounding darkness might only catch a glimpse of an enormous, dark-furred beast as he raced by. Even so, I knew Max would never let himself be seen or photographed like that unless it was absolutely necessary. He wasn't acting like the wise, experienced man I knew. Whatever spell Malleus had thrown at him appeared to be clouding his reasoning. In his wolf form, he might well have gone even farther away from his usual logic circuits in favor of ripping me limb from limb. *Wonderful,* I thought, with as much sarcasm as I could muster. And I can muster a lot of it.

If he were conscious, I was sure Malleus would find all this amusing. I glared at Ariana, though I was truly glaring at the hateful man within her body. I didn't mind getting hurt in a fight, but these were my friends. I had so few. First chance I got, I planned to rip Malleus into as many pieces as possible, but I wanted him in his own body first.

Glancing in the rearview mirror, I caught another flash of dark fur and lightning-fast movement. I needed to get Max out of plain sight. If he wasn't in full control of himself, then I needed to protect him. I found that hilarious, especially since I was barely keeping it together myself under the influence of the bone cuffs. It was a close thing, minute by minute. *I'll be damned if I let Malleus control me like that again, though. Nope. No way.* Bargain or no bargain, he didn't own me. Not where it counted. I focused on getting my breathing under control as I whipped the car around a turn. *And I'm not letting that asshole hurt Max either.*

The place I sought wasn't far away, a building that used to be an electronics store. When the pandemic rolled through, it took a surprising number of big businesses along with it, and companies that had been alive and kicking for half a century or more had gone the way of the dodo. As sad as that was, it gave me an opportunity—a place where I could have both space and privacy to deal with this situation. I passed a silent cop car at an intersection, but the officer inside didn't even flick his eyes my way as I hurtled by. Realizing I had an enormous beast pursuing me in full view in the street, I hurriedly tossed an illusion his way to make him unnoticed. I craned my neck as Max passed in front of the same vehicle, but no red and blue lights came on. The car pulled out and turned the opposite direction, leaving me to breathe a sigh of relief.

You owe me one for keeping the cops away, Max. Even as I finished the thought, I dismissed it just as quickly. He didn't owe me anything. He was as much a victim of Malleus as Ariana and I. I cut my eyes towards Ariana and wished Malleus was in his own body so I could end this whole thing with one swipe of my claws. I sighed and turned my eyes to the road. *One thing at a time,* I thought. *We'll get through this mess.*

Pushing the car hard, I made my way south. I took a sharp left underneath a freeway and looked back to see that I'd managed to put a little space between us and Max, though not nearly as much as I'd have liked. Once we reached our destination, I'd still have to move fast to get Ariana's body out of the car and into the building I had in mind.

One more right turn, followed by a quick left, brought me into a roughly paved field that served as a loading area for the empty store. I swerved around a couple of huge potholes and skidded to a stop next to one of the rear entrances, keeping an eye out for Max. I hopped out and grabbed Ariana from the passenger seat, slinging her over my shoulder again. She'd hate that I carried her all over town like a sack of flour, but I had no choice. I hustled up to the nearest access door, which was locked as I knew it would be. Fortunately, one of my built-in abilities is my way with simple locks. It's a thing. It took a moment to get focused, but once I got my magick flowing, the locks popped open at my call, easy as you please.

Thank the Goddess for small favors, I thought as I yanked open the door and slipped inside. As I pulled the door closed, I heard a low, menacing growl somewhere far behind me. Glancing over my shoulder, I caught a glimpse of a huge, dark shape as it rounded the corner a few hundred yards away. I pulled the door all the way closed and reengaged the locks, though I knew they'd not last long against Max's strength. *He's persistent, that one.*

Still carrying Ariana's body, I raced across the windowless storeroom that made up the back part of the store and slipped through an opening into what had been the shopping floor. They had yet to remove all the shelving. Although there were a few displays piled up against one wall near the front, they hadn't finished moving everything out, so I had to dodge through the empty rows near the back of the store. I emerged into a larger open space near the front and saw doors to a few smaller showrooms and offices lining either wall. Boards covered the huge front windows, but a hint of illumination from the moon filtered down through an array of circular skylights high overhead. The place had otherwise been emptied out, and a thick coat of dust covered the floor. Back in the warehouse area, something huge slammed into the locked door I'd come through. The sound echoed as the shock dislodged drifts of dust from the ceiling.

Picking a door that seemed to lead to an enclosed office, I yanked it open and slipped into the smaller chamber. Aside from thick shadows, the room contained only a huge empty desk, some shelves, and a chair. I laid Ariana's body down on the desk's surface. I placed my hand on her head and grimaced, knowing what I had to do and not liking it. If Malleus woke up, he'd be free to run around in Ariana's body and continue causing trouble for me. I'd have all I could handle with Max, so I knew the only way I could bind her was with magick. Malleus would never let me do it if he was conscious, but if I went in too deeply, he'd awaken and fight back. I had to be subtle.

Not my strong suit, I thought, but nevertheless, bent myself to the task. Keeping my magickal intrusion as light as I could, I passed along the suggestion of calm, rest and sleep. For a moment, I felt the oily touch of Malleus's awareness, but only faintly, and I continued my work. Already relaxed, I saw Ariana's body settle even more, and her head rolled off to one side, her mouth dropping open. I'd seen Ariana fall asleep on numerous occasions, and seeing her move now, even in sleep, struck a warning chord in me. It didn't look right, not proper at all. *That's because it's not Ariana who's sleeping,* I

119

thought, *it's Malleus.* I examined Ariana's pretty face and noted that it had taken on a hard look, even in slumber. That wasn't her. I'd seen her angry as hell, but even when she was fighting with everything she had, kicking ass after ass, she still showed a softness, something sweet. I shook my head to clear it. *Damn cuffs making me emotional.* I checked Ariana's shackles, making sure they were still secure.

From the back of the store came the wrenching scream of tortured metal, followed by an animal howl of rage. *Max.* I sighed. I'd have to fight him, no way around that, at least until I could calm him down somehow. After that, all I had to do was get him back to his human form so he wouldn't kill me, then find a way to get Malleus to remove my cuffs and cancel his bargain, all in fairly short order. *Dammit,* I thought. I usually love a challenge, but these stakes were high. My friends shouldn't have to suffer because of me. The thought of seeing Ariana's body possessed by a truly evil person, and killing Max, infuriated me.

Something stirred in me, then, something I wasn't used to feeling at all. Anger, that was already in full force. Determination, check. I'd been through stuff far worse than this, so I was confident I'd get through it one way or another. But there was something different forming down there in my heart of hearts, a cold, hollow spot that had never been there before. It gnawed at me, an ache that I couldn't immediately place. When I realized what it was, I thought about fighting it, but the truth is that I knew I didn't want to. The cuffs were pushing me, yes, but what I felt was beneath all that. It was real. The cuffs only brought it out and made me confront it.

I sighed, closed my eyes, and allowed myself to give it voice, to finally acknowledge it by sending a whisper of my will into the ether.

Avery. Avy, I thought, *I need you. Come to me.*

Chapter 13

Avery parked the Jeep a block away, drew her gun, and kept to the shadows as she made her way to Bell, Book, and Cauldron. She noted that the little red car that had occupied a parking spot in the front was gone and guessed that Malleus had made off with it. She imagined Ariana's body leaving the shop, hopping in the car, and driving away with Malleus in charge, and it made her blood boil. *Stay cool,* she thought, *I could be wrong. He might still be in there*. Letting her training dictate her movements, she skirted the parking lot and stalked along the front of the building until she could survey the interior without being seen from within.

The shop was still a shambles, but Avery could tell that the shop girl, Lorena, had made progress in cleaning up the mess. Avery scanned the room, but saw no sign of the young woman, nor of Cyrus. Confident that there was no immediate danger, she moved forward and tried the door. Unlocked. She pushed it open and slipped inside.

"Cyrus?" she called, hoping the old man was alive. She picked her way through the debris until she heard a muffled thumping from one side of the store. She swiveled in the direction of the noise, gun aimed. "Who's there?" The only answer was more thumping.

The noise became clearer as Avery approached. She turned down one aisle and saw a closed door in the wall at the far end, probably a closet. The door rattled from an impact as she watched, and a garbled female voice drifted out from within.

"Don't move!" she called out. "Police! I'm going to open the door. I'm armed. Do you understand me?"

There was a pause, quickly followed by two sharp raps, then silence.

Avery sidled up to the door and waited a second before flinging it open. She found a broom closet filled with cleaning supplies, along with the purple-haired shop girl, secured to a chair with a copious amount of duct tape. The girl's eyes widened as she stared at Avery's gun, and she remained still as a sculpture.

"Lorena! Are you hurt?" Avery said as she holstered her sidearm.

The girl shook her head and sighed behind her gag, relieved. Avery whipped a folding knife from her pocket and cut the silvery tape away. The instant her hands were free, Lorena reached up and untied the scarf Malleus had used as a gag.

"No, I'm ok! That blonde woman—I thought she was nice! Then she came out of Cyrus's office, punched me in the face, and tied me up in here! That bitch! I'd have kicked her ass if she hadn't sucker punched me like that, but wow, she hit hard."

Avery winced as she noticed the swelling that had arisen around Lorena's left eye. She hesitated a moment, wondering how much to reveal, but decided on the truth. "It wasn't her fault. She was possessed by a sorcerer, a very bad man. We're trying to catch him now."

Lorena's eyes widened. "Really? Wow, big yikes! So that wasn't her?"

Avery shook her head. "Not exactly, no. Her body, but not her spirit. Are you all right?"

Lorena nodded. "Yeah, I'll be fine. I used to be in the roller derby, I'm used to getting knocked around. How's Cyrus? Is he all right?"

"I don't know. Where is he?"

"He was in his conjuring room with her! He's probably still in there!" Lorena jumped to her feet, but then swayed and put a hand on the doorframe to steady herself. "Whoa, room's a little spinny..."

Avery took her by the arms and sat her back down. "Sit here for a minute, get yourself together. I'll go check on Cyrus."

"But he might be hurt!"

"Yes, and it might still be dangerous. I've got this. It won't take a moment, just stay here. I'll call out for you when it's safe. Don't go anywhere, okay?"

Lorena nodded reluctantly and sat back in the chair, fear for Cyrus showing on her face.

Avery drew her gun again and left the closet, heading for Cyrus's conjuring room. The door had been left open. A quick peek revealed Cyrus lying face-down on the wooden planks, unmoving. *No blood. At least none I can see,* Avery thought as she pressed her back up against the wall next to the door.

"Cyrus!" Avery called out. "It's Detective Lynne! Are you all right? Is anyone in there with you?" No reply. She took a deep breath, readied her gun, and slipped into the room.

It took only a couple of seconds for her to see that they were alone, and she holstered her gun again as she bent to examine Cyrus. His pulse was strong, and Avery sighed with relief. He groaned at her touch and began to stir. A lump had formed on the back of his head. Avery carefully helped him roll over.

"Take it slowly, there, man. He hit you with something."

With Avery's help, Cyrus pushed himself into a seated position, grimacing in pain. He squinted his eyes shut and opened them again a few times as he tried to focus. When he spoke, he sounded much older than he had at their first meeting.

"Ah, I'm so sorry, detective. I didn't see that coming."

"Obviously," Avery chuckled, patting him on the shoulder. "It's okay, we couldn't have known. He took you by surprise. All of us, actually."

"Wait—he?"

Avery realized that he didn't yet know what had happened. "It happened during Ariana's attempt to break the tracking spell Malleus was using to keep tabs on Kane. She broke the connection, all right, but somehow, their spirits got transferred along that connection before the link disappeared. Ariana's spirit is stuck in Malleus's body, but Kane said she's a prisoner in there. She can feel everything that's going on, but she can't DO anything. It's like the body's in a coma, but she's awake inside. Meanwhile, Malleus has completely taken over Ariana's body and is driving it like a rental car."

Cyrus turned astonished eyes towards Avery as she explained. When she'd finished, he held himself silent for a few seconds before answering.

"What an utter. . .bastard!"

"I couldn't agree more," Avery concurred. She hesitated, then plunged forward, hoping for the best. "Can you switch them back?"

Cyrus was probing the knot on the back of his skull and grimacing in pain. "Ow. What? Oh, yes, I can do that. It's difficult, but not impossible."

"You've done this before?"

Cyrus's eyes flicked away and Avery caught a touch of embarrassment in them at first. "Well. . .no." His narrow chest swelled as he found his former dignity. "But I don't know that you have a lot of old wizards to choose from just now, do you?" Avery remained silent, and Cyrus continued, a note of pride seeping into his voice, "I may not seem like much to young eyes, but I've seen and done things that would curl your hair, lass. I can do this little trick. I just need. . .let me see, what do I need?" He pushed himself to his feet, his movements becoming more assured as he contemplated the task before him.

Cyrus walked to a nearby cabinet, pulled a set of keys from his pocket, and unlocked a drawer. From within, he pulled a dark wooden box, which he also unlocked. Moving with exaggerated care, he removed an ancient-looking leather-bound book, set it on the desk, and opened it. He winced, then uttered a few syllables and held out his palm. A gentle blue fire sprang from his hand, and he pressed the flame into the knot on the back of his head, chanting quietly. The flame seeped into his skin and disappeared. When he removed his hand, the knot had vanished. He looked over his shoulder at Avery and smiled.

"See? Quite a few tricks up my sleeve. Oh, Lorena, I'm glad you're here, come help me, we need a few things."

Avery turned to find Lorena peeking into the room with wide eyes. She was about to reprimand her for not staying put, but just shook her head. She figured they needed all the help they could get.

When he caught sight of her bruised face, Cyrus gasped. "My stars, girl, what happened? Never mind, come here, let me fix that." Lorena hesitated only a moment, then cautiously moved forward to stand in front of her boss, eyes wide. Cyrus repeated the blue fire spell and Lorena's swelling disappeared.

"Wow, that's so COOL!" Lorena exclaimed, astonished and excited.

"Yes, yes, I'm happy to help," Cyrus said, but Avery saw him sag, leaning forward to rest his hands heavily on his desk as though he'd just run a mile. He sighed, revealing his weariness, but still kept a glimmer of a pleased smile.

Magick costs. Avery remembered Ariana's words from a lesson. *It'll wear you out, so you need to be careful. Use too much, and you could even...you know, die. So, watch it.* "Are you all right, Cyrus?"

Cyrus didn't answer right away but took up a pen and scribbled on a pad. Without looking up, he grumbled, "Am I all right? Why wouldn't I be? I've just had my business demolished by a demon, been knocked unconscious by a body-hopping thug, and now I'm apparently going to fling myself headlong into Goddess-knows-what kind of mayhem alongside a damned GrimFaerie! I'm just peachy, Detective. Peachy, I say!" Then he sighed, as if resigning himself to the whole mess, tore off the sheet and handed it to Lorena. His voice softened as he spoke to her, "Go and get these things for me, my dear, and be careful with the last two. They're...touchy." The girl took the list, read it, and looked back at Cyrus uncertainly. "Yes, I know, just get them. They're in the locked cabinet in the wall, the big one."

Shaking her head, she turned to go, her words drifting over her shoulder as she left the room, "You got it boss."

Still reading from the book, Cyrus addressed Avery, "We'll need to get their bodies close together, no more than a few yards if necessary. Unless we can link them together with something." He smiled and squinted at Avery, a sly gleam appearing in his eye, "I've got an idea about that. Where's Malleus's body now?"

"In the Jeep," Avery replied with a touch of embarrassment. "I hated to leave it like that, knowing Ariana's in there, but that was the best I could do. The body is secured, in case Malleus suddenly comes back into it, but it's fine." She frowned. "How are we going to find Ariana's body? And Kane, how will we find him?"

Cyrus pointed to the pillow on the floor within the casting circle nearby. "Check that for Ariana's hair. Even one strand will be enough for me to form a tracking spell that will take us right to her body. Kane? Well, he's beyond my reach, but I'm betting he won't be far from her. He's got a knack for trouble, and I'm sure we'll find him soon enough. Ah, thank you." He accepted the hairs Avery had found on the pillow. "All right then, let's get to work."

Twenty minutes later, they exited the store. Cyrus set down the duffle he carried and locked the door behind them. "Lorena, dear, go on home, and please keep all this to yourself. I'm so sorry you got hurt tonight. This has definitely been above and beyond anything I could have expected from you." He turned to face her and sighed, "If you decide to look for work elsewhere, I completely understand."

Lorena gasped. "Quit? Not on your life!" The girl laughed, startling both Cyrus and Avery. "I haven't had this much fun, like, *ever*. I'll be in tomorrow!" She threw a dazzling smile, "But I won't turn down that hazard pay we talked about, that's for sure."

Cyrus started in surprise but recovered quickly, "Indeed. We'll handle it tomorrow. Go on, then, stay safe. And again, not a word to anyone."

She crossed her heart, paused, and leaned in close, surprising Cyrus with a brief hug and a peck on the cheek. "Stay safe, old man. I want my bonus!" She bounced off to a light blue moped chained to a tree nearby. She donned an enormous white helmet and was on her way in moments, tossing a wave over her shoulder as she buzzed away.

"Spunky girl you've got there," Avery observed.

"I had no idea. I just hired her because she knew a few things about tarot cards and was willing to work nights and weekends."

"Not because she's cute and curvy?"

Cyrus blinked twice before answering, embarrassment coloring his pale face. "I'm old, Detective, but I'm not dead. She certainly is both of those things, which is great for business. Even so, I have no designs on her, I'm old enough to be her great grandfather. And besides, I've already got a girlfriend. Two, if I'm to be honest."

Avery's mouth dropped open to respond, but her words never made it out. A wave of longing and urgency swept through her body, making her skin prickle with goosebumps. She gasped at the intensity of it.

Avery. Avy, Kane's voice echoed in her mind, *I need you. Come to me.*

The power of his words reverberated through every fiber of her being, galvanizing her. Her heartbeat thumped in her ears, threatening to overpower her other senses. His words, so few but infused with longing and urgency, both elated and scared her. Despite her fear, she knew she'd answer that call no matter what it took. The world spun, and she tried to stand firm in the middle of it.

Cyrus laid a hand on her shoulder to steady her. "What is it? Are you all right?"

Caught up in the power of what had just happened, Avery took a moment to be sure she wouldn't garble her words before she turned to Cyrus, "We've got to go. Now. Kane needs me. Us. He needs us right away."

Cyrus nodded, the determination in his face making him look less like a doddering old scholar and more like a grizzled veteran. "Indeed. Let's go." He turned to look around the lot and frowned. "Wait, where's my car?"

Chapter 14

Werewolves are strong, quick, and have a sense of smell that you wouldn't believe. They're also natural fighters, using claws and fangs to good effect. They're bigger and stronger than me, and ferocious to a fault. I've fought a few in my day, and each time, I've come away with a few more scars. Even scars made by demons fade in time from my body, but werewolf scars don't. They stick around, though I have no idea why. Maybe as a reminder that I should keep my wits about me when dealing with them.

The ceiling of the empty store left the supports exposed, presenting a wide expanse of monkey bars for someone like me. I clambered up the wall until I could reach them, then swung myself hand-over-hand until I was centered over the open space in the front of the store. There, I settled myself in to wait. I knew I wouldn't have to wait long.

A roar of anger came from the shadows in back of the store, then a long, low growl that tapered into silence.

Uh, oh, I thought. I held myself as still as a stone, opening up my senses to the full, but kept my magick to myself. If I sent a trailer of magick out looking for Max, I'd find him, all right. And he'd find me just as quickly. Instead, I watched, listened, and waited. Silence fell throughout the empty store.

Minutes slowly ticked by. *Be patient. He's there.* At last, I caught a glimpse of movement. I narrowed my eyes, scanning the shelves that bordered the far wall, wanting to be sure of what I saw. When he emerged, I wondered how the hell he could have been so stealthy.

In werewolf form, Max was enormous. A big man to begin with, he bulked up tremendously when he wolfed out. Even so, there was none of the clumsiness I'd seen

129

with similarly large creatures. Trolls, ogres, and goblins all tended to bump into things at every turn. Not Max.

At first, I only saw a hint of movement in the dark, along with the faintest of sniffing sounds, but then he emerged from the shadows in truly impressive fashion.

He approached on all fours, hiding behind the array of empty shelves, but once he moved clear of them, he stood to his full height and glory. I noted again the thick cords of muscle that covered his body beneath the black and grey wolf pelt. Bulging, muscular arms a touch too long ended in hands tipped with wickedly sharp nails that I'd seen go through steel plate. Max clenched and unclenched his hands as if imagining how he would attack me. It looked like it would hurt. He'd easily separate my upper half from my lower if he got a good enough grip. He took in a breath and let it out, the sound deep and powerful. His fangs were as long as my little finger, and there were plenty of other teeth besides. Ouch.

He scanned everything with those golden amber eyes, his head moving back and forth, not missing a thing. Well, he missed me, but I was up pretty high, and I knew he'd spot me sooner or later. As it looked like going hand-to-hand was riskier then even I preferred, I decided to try subtlety before strength and hope for the best.

One of my abilities as a GrimFaerie was casting illusions. Some illusions could stand on their own. They were things unto themselves that automatically interacted with anyone who perceived them. If I desired, I could create an illusion that looked like a person or thing, park it somewhere, and anyone who saw it for the next hour or two would remember it as I'd intended. Veils were similar, not needing my direction once they were created, only requiring me to keep energy flowing to them. I could do those in my sleep.

The best illusions, though, were deeply immersive experiences created in the viewer's mind. Far more than just a visual experience, that kind of illusion included smell, taste, touch, every sense they had. Those were as real as real could get. Took a bit more effort though. And the stronger the mind, the more difficult the job. The minds of ordinary humans were like toys to me unless they had training. Sorcerers and witches were harder to fool. Ancient werewolves with centuries to discipline their minds enough to become billionaire philanthropists, and under the influence of an aggression-enhancing spell? Piece of cake. Crap cake, that is.

Emotions are energy, and if I had to put up with Malleus's cuffs pushing me to be more aggressive, then I figured I could use that to my advantage. Keeping my mind on the spell I wanted to cast, I let some of my internal chains go, allowing my anger, my lust, my hunger to emerge, flooding me with the desire to fling myself down on my enemy. *My friend,* I forcefully corrected myself as I clenched my teeth, testing the limits of my internal discipline. Once I got a handle on it, I gathered up those raging feelings, that barely controlled energy, and molded it all into something I could use. My body quivered with the effort, but I somehow kept my mind right, stayed focused, and with a gesture of my right hand, I sent the illusion spell flying towards the powerful wolfman down below.

Although there was nothing physical about my attack, Max staggered as though I'd hit him in the head with a cannonball. The huge creature fell on its side, clutching its head, growling in surprise and frustration. I poured more energy into my spell, and his struggles slowed. Seconds passed, and he pushed himself up on his elbows to look around. His growls faded, and he fell silent but for his heavy breathing. The big head shook once, then again, and the werewolf surveyed the empty, darkened room, seeing not the dusty tiles and shadowed emptiness, but instead seeing what I willed him to see.

Max found himself in a beautiful meadow on a mountainside. The sun shone warmly down, the scent of flowers drifted on a gentle breeze, and the comforting sound of a distant waterfall mingled with the sweetest birdsongs. His head tilted skyward to see the bluest of blue skies, complete with cotton ball clouds hanging lazily on the air. There were no enemies to fight. This place felt secure and safe, a paradise of serenity, peace, and calm.

I sensed Max's powerful heartbeat begin to slow as the tranquility of the scene began to do its work. He blinked a few times, then got to his feet, slowly turning around, taking in the sights, the smells, everything. His massive shoulders relaxed, he stood up out of his fighting crouch, and his breathing evened out. The desire to fight slowly drained away.

"It's a trap!" Ariana's harsh voice echoed throughout the building, destroying everything I'd built in Max's mindscape, "He's trying to kill you! He's up there!"

Max whipped his head towards the voice. When he couldn't see its source, he squeezed his eyes shut and shook his head several times, grunting and growling. When they opened again, they were focused and once again seeing truly. Malleus had somehow sidestepped my magickal binding, escaped the handcuffs, and stood in the doorway. And he was pointing at me. I felt my illusion snap as Max broke free of it, and I glanced down only to see the werewolf's burning amber eyes fixed on me.

That's not good. I sighed, knowing what came next. A part of me hated to do it, but I can't deny that a bigger part of me was eager to move on to Plan B. *Time to pick up some more scars.* I let go of the joists and pushed with my legs, flinging myself down towards an angry werewolf.

I knew Max could see through a veil, but I could still make him see other things. As I dropped through the air towards him, I created bright bursts of light before his eyes, making him blink in surprise an instant before I hit him. The impact was like hitting a furry brick wall, but I caught a lucky break for a change. I felt him shift, momentarily putting all his weight on his right foot, and I knew I'd caught him off balance. Capitalizing on the move, I grabbed his neck with both arms and put all my strength into a vicious twist as I reached the floor. He actually uttered a Scooby Doo noise of surprise when his feet left the tiles, as if shocked to find himself airborne and flying across the room. Strength matters, but technique can make a big difference, and I've been doing this a long time.

The impact wouldn't hurt him, but at least it gave me some time and space to get to Malleus. Before Max crashed into the wall, I was already on the move. The shadows were in my favor, for even though I knew the sorcerer could see through my veil if he looked hard enough, darkness made that more difficult, and my darting, zig-zag movements compounded the difficulty.

I knew I was on the right track when a blast of energy exploded off to my left. I juked back in that direction, and sure enough, another blast erupted near where I'd just been. He blasted away randomly, hoping he'd catch me. My Fae eyesight cut through the shadows to see Ariana's pretty face screwed into a scowl full of malice that was definitely not hers.

"Just kill him!" Malleus screamed in her voice. "Kill the werewolf and you're free!" Another blast of force lanced from her outstretched fingers and took out a corner of a nearby office, blasting sheetrock everywhere. "That was the deal! Do you want to be more of a freak than you already are? Just do it!" Another blast of power, nowhere near me this time. I smiled. I was getting closer. I flattened myself to the floor, gathered my feet under me, and prepared to spring across the open space to tackle the body of my best friend.

I've mentioned that werewolves are fast, right? I should have kept that fact in the forefront of my mind as I worked my way towards Malleus. Max hit me like a freight train, knocking the wind out of me and taking us both through the nearest office wall. His talons dug deeply into the flesh of my back and stomach where he'd wrapped his arms around me, and unbearable pain shot through me. That's when we hit the steel column that stood next to the outer wall. If I thought I hurt before, that impact proved I had vastly underestimated my capacity for pain—that new agony was transcendent. Wow.

I grabbed the nearest hairy index finger I could reach and snapped it back as hard as I could. It cracked like a tree branch, and Max roared in my ear as he instinctively let go of me, yanking the injured limb away and cradling it close to his body. Gritting my teeth against the nauseating pain in my torso, I tossed another of my bright flash illusions in front of his face, this time sending more power to it and adding sharp firecracker noises for good measure. I willed the spell to keep going for a couple of minutes, hoping to distract him long enough for me to escape. He roared in frustration as he flung a hairy arm up over his eyes and swatted ineffectually at the flashing lights that only he could see, shaking his head as the noise assaulted him as well.

Taking that as my cue to exit, I tried to sprint through the hole in the wall we'd just made, but my legs refused to function properly. My back was on fire, the pain blinding, and something felt jangly and disconnected inside me. I was a marionette with janky strings, my legs ignoring every plea of mine to just do their usual thing. I'm sure that had to have happened before, but for the life of me, I couldn't remember when. I could barely keep myself upright, and I had to admit I was growing concerned.

I stumbled to the opening, intending to blast through it and find something resembling cover, but I tripped and fell in the debris near the wall, slamming my face into the dusty floor just outside the office. I barely felt that pain amongst all the rest. The familiar popping sensations in my back began as my body started to put itself to rights, but it would be painful, and would take longer than I really had. I willed my body to fix itself faster, even while knowing that nothing could rush that process.

A pair of all too familiar boots appeared a few inches away from me. I'd seen Ariana wear those boots a hundred times. Hell, she'd worn them the night we'd first met. Seeing them at that moment, though, did nothing to lift my spirits. I tilted my head and peered upwards only to see an ugly sneer I'd never seen from Ariana, but I'm sure it looked at home on Malleus's true face. He was pointing one of Ariana's guns at my head. In my battered state, I wasn't entirely sure I could survive a few headshots from so close. I hated to admit it, but I knew there was almost nothing I could do but freeze.

"You couldn't just do the job, could you?" Ariana's voice dripped with disgust. "The legendary GrimFaerie, can't even take out a simple werewolf. Pathetic. You deserve to lose your hands."

I stared up at him, struggling with the agony of my broken back as well as the assault on my emotions from the cuffs. It took everything I had to just stay sane at that point. *Stall him,* I thought. I needed both answers and time, and bad guys always love to talk. I gritted my teeth and hoped he was more egotistical than practical.

"Yeah, I suck. He's too tough for me. But why go to all this trouble? Must have taken weeks to build these cuffs. Why drag me into this?"

"Oh, is this where I reveal my evil plan before I kill you?" Malleus smirked, keeping the gun trained on my forehead.

I hoped he couldn't hear the bones in my back struggling to pop themselves back in order. The pain finally diminished to something manageable, but it was still hard to breathe. I groaned, making it look like I was still in unbearable agony.

"Worth a try." I shrugged. "I'm curious. Doesn't hurt you to tell me if I'm about to die anyway, right?"

Malleus laughed, "I suppose you're right. Yes, think I will." A smug smile wormed its way across Ariana's face. "Elias Bress sends his regards."

I blinked in surprise. I thought Elias Bress was long gone, but it seemed I was wrong. Oddly, Elias had been the reason I'd met Ariana and Max in the first place. Bress was a rich businessman operating out of Houston a couple of years ago. He was also a murderer, responsible for the deaths of twelve women that I knew of. When he'd sent one of his men to abduct and kill Ariana to complete a magickal working of his, the Goddess had sent me to put a stop to it. One thing led to another and we stormed the high rise he'd used as a headquarters. We hadn't known Bress had imprisoned Max there, but we found him and set him free. In the end, we'd run Bress out of town, but not before Ariana had put a bullet in his right hand. I looked down at mine, my wrists still bearing the bone cuffs. Sometimes, Karma forgot who the good guys were.

"He said both of your hands would almost be worth one of his. Payback's a bitch, isn't it? I needed information, and Elias was very forthcoming. His only condition was that I use you as the tool to extract my revenge. He wanted both you and Ariana to suffer." He smiled with Ariana's lips and I marveled at how unlike her it looked. I'd bet her lips had never sneered like that in her life. "As for Gerhardt in there, I've got my reasons.

Since it looks like I can't trust you to see this through, I guess I should be glad that your girl uses enchanted rounds. Enough of these will put Gerhardt out of my misery, and I'll still have enough left over for you." He made a show of thinking something over. "Although, I may still let you live out your days as a handless, magickless assassin and see how that works out for you. That could be amusing in the long term, and Bress will be happy either way. Ah well, I can worry about that later."

His eyes lifted from mine as he searched for Max, and the gun raised a moment later as he sighted in on the stricken werewolf behind me. Malleus tightened Ariana's finger on the trigger.

Fortunately for me, Ariana hated steel-toed boots. She favored mobility over armor as far as her feet went. I hated to do it, but desperate situations and all that. The claws on the middle two fingers of my right hand slid easily through the thick leather of her left boot and continued through the unprotected foot within. Judging from the awful scream of surprise and agony that erupted from Ariana's mouth, I guessed it hurt.

I rolled to my right as the gun went off above me, the bullets pockmarking the tiles where I'd been an instant before, and I rolled back and slapped the gun from Malleus's hand. It slid across the floor and into the shadows, making a hideous scraping sound along the way.

First I stab her in the foot, then I scratch up one of her precious guns. She's gonna be pissed when she gets her body back, I thought.

I glanced back at Max and saw that he was unharmed, and still struggling to free his vision of my strobelight spell. He'd also heard the shots, and although I doubted any had hit him, even in his frenzied state he instinctively shied away from the gunfire. He ducked behind the nearest wall, still swatting at the lights that assailed him.

Malleus scrambled away from me, grunting in agony and leaving a thin trail of Ariana's blood on the floor. He still had Ariana's other gun strapped to his left thigh, but for the moment, he seemed to be ignoring it in favor of putting some space between us. Seeing him crawling backwards like that, injured and vulnerable, made my predatory instincts leap to the fore. I started towards him, ready to rip and tear and bite, my emotions surging as the cuffs influence took hold. I caught a glimpse of her eyes, wide and finally afraid. That did it. I checked myself and stopped my forward motion. It wasn't easy.

That's Ariana's body, I thought. *Damn, I nearly ripped it to shreds just now.* I forced myself to calm down enough to think. *Have to find another way.* I took a precious few seconds to consider what I knew about Malleus, the ways I'd seen him use his magick. Every sorcerer has identifiable patterns in how they apply their skills the same way that different musicians could play the very same instrument and yet produce completely different and distinctive music. Malleus was strong and disciplined. *So why hasn't he hit me with more stuff?* I thought. *He could have blasted me with magick just now but chose Ariana's gun instead. Why?*

I thought about the magick bolts he'd thrown at me earlier and realized that they weren't that strong. Certainly weaker than I'd expected them to be. *Why?* The answer hit me. His skills were physical as much as they were mental. The mind-to-body connection is an integral part of magick, and you must truly know yourself, inside and out, to reach high levels of mastery. I recalled the scars I'd seen on Malleus's true form and realized that he'd never be as powerful in Ariana's body as he was in his own. Even though his knowledge was there, he didn't know Ariana's body well enough, couldn't feel his way through the more intricate spells the way he could if he were in his own shell. He'd bound his mind to that body with hours of intense ritual, a great abundance of pain and suffering, and he knew every inch of his own tortured skin intimately. Ariana's body was a mystery to him. He wasn't working at full capacity. He was still dangerous, but less than he was before.

I smiled. Things were looking up.

Chapter 15

While Malleus was dealing with his pain, I wove my way through the empty shelves, gradually regaining coordination in my legs as I went. When I slipped through the doors into the loading area, I was still figuring out how to get the drop on him when something bounced into the room behind me and exploded. Flashbangs are loud as hell, and I was close enough that the overpressure staggered me. Malleus had apparently brought a few more of Ariana's favorite toys. I'd been in too much of a hurry to search her body, and I knew she stashed all kinds of goodies on her person.

I stumbled away from the blast site and looked at the ceiling again. It was easy enough to leap up, grab the steel supports, and hoist myself up to perch among them. Malleus had seen me do it once, but now he was hurt, and he had Max freaking out just a few yards away. I reached out with my magick to get a sense of the werewolf's attitude and ran smack into a swirl of pissed-off-edness the likes of which should have won Max a medal.

Fortunately, he still couldn't do much while my strobe-and-sound spell kept him occupied. Even so, he wouldn't be distracted for long, and I figured I only had a minute or two before he figured something out and either came after me or made himself a target for Malleus.

I hit on an idea and figured the worst that could happen wouldn't leave me in any worse shape. My ears were still ringing from the grenade, and I was already fatigued, but even so, it was worth a shot.

As Ariana might say, I gathered some serious chi, then carefully tapped into the illusion I'd left with Max. Once I had the connection formed, I began to add a stronger foundation to it, shoring up the quick-and-dirty flash spell and giving it some heft and weight I could build upon. Once the foundation was laid, I opened up and poured power into it, expanding it, hitting it with everything I had. I needed this to work. The effort left me woozy, but the spell seemed to be functional. I checked it over one last time. *That's as good as I can make it.* I detached myself from the spell and tried to catch my breath. That took longer than I liked, but once I was steady enough, I returned my attention to Malleus. He needed an ass whooping in the worst way.

Keeping silent, I climbed through the supports until I was directly over the big doors I'd just come through. I waited a few seconds, then slowly leaned over until my line of sight cleared the top of the opening. Hanging upside down like a bat and allowing as little of myself to be seen as I could, I surveyed the battleground.

Malleus was on his feet (Ariana's feet, anyway) again, though he was leaning hard on one of the shelving units in obvious pain. As much as I hated damaging Ariana's body like that, knowing Malleus was feeling it made me smile. He gritted his teeth against it and managed to get Ariana's other gun out of the holster on her left hip. He racked a round into the chamber and trained it on the opening below me.

"Hide if you like! I'll kill whichever of you I see first, it makes no difference to me! I win either way!"

Throwing your voice is easy when you're a GrimFaerie. They don't actually hear the sound with their ears since the spell puts my voice directly into their mind, and that gives me a lot of leeway. It's a tiny enough spell to be beneath Malleus's notice. At this point in the fight, he'd expect something bigger. I focused my magick and sent a whisper of it across the room. Too much power, and he'd follow it back to the source, but if I kept it light. . .

"You're not getting away from here," my voice, cold and menacing, drifted out of a far corner. Malleus whipped his head around and peered into the darkness, searching for me. I moved my voice a few yards to the left. "I'm going to rip you apart, Malleus. Literally."

"Sure you will," he sneered. He scanned the room, slowly moving the barrel of the gun along his line of sight as he searched for any telltale signs of my presence. "I'm sure you'll love getting your claws into your old friend here. You've probably been dreaming of it for months. I know your kind."

I sent a few stealthy sounds, a quiet scuff of foot on tile, a thump, a faint breath. Malleus hunched his shoulders as he strained to see. *Good,* I thought, *he's buying it for now.* I added a layer of cover to my distraction, masking any sounds I made and adding more noises elsewhere to make him think I was across the building. Malleus shifted his position to take cover behind one of the shelves, his back towards me, and I lowered myself from my hiding spot and dropped to the floor below.

"Whatever Bress told you of my kind is probably wrong," my disembodied voice taunted him from across the room as I crept through the maze of shelving towards his unprotected back. "It's probably just as well you sought me out. One of us would have come for you sooner or later anyway." I paused for a moment, drawing out the conversation, "I am a little confused, though. It makes perfect sense that Bress would want me and Ariana to suffer. I get that. But his interest in Max was never personal. Bress just wanted something Max had. Why the hell would you want him dead? He's actually a decent guy."

I felt the energy as he released it. I tensed to dive for cover, but it wasn't an attack at all. Malleus had grown tired of the shadows. A brightly glowing sphere the size of a basketball rose to the ceiling, giving off a pale illumination that chased away the darkness in the empty store. I ducked a little closer to the nearest display, taking what cover I could, but no further action was taken. The globe pulsed and vibrated with energy, stopping its ascent when it bumped into the rafters up above.

"Because he deserves to die!" Malleus screamed in a hateful version of Ariana's voice. The pain seemed to have eroded some of Malleus's composure. "He—my father—it's all von Gerhardt's fault!"

I'd finally touched a nerve. *Now we're getting somewhere,* I thought. Homing in on Malleus's location, I worked my way forward again. I covered half the floor between us, and if I could keep him occupied a while longer, I'd have him.

"Max did something to your father." I made it a statement rather than a question, moving my voice around the far side of the room.

"Of course!" Malleus spat. "My father was a good man. He didn't deserve what that rich bastard did to him!" He grunted in pain, and I heard him slam his back up against the outer wall of a nearby office. "My father died because of Gerhardt! And now the high and mighty Maximus will pay for what he did!"

As I crept closer, I created the tiniest illusion in a far corner of the store, no more than a ripple in the air that might have been something. Malleus squeezed off two shots in that direction. I threw another illusion a few yards closer to Malleus than the first, and he fired again. Ariana's voice was ragged as Malleus used it to scream in frustration. Pain and blood loss were getting to him.

I was still a few yards away when I heard the door to the office slam shut and then lock. I glared at it, knowing it wouldn't keep me out for more than a few seconds, but charging a cornered sorcerer is generally not wise, and I needed to check on Max. Keeping myself veiled, I dodged around the shelves until I came to the opening of the smaller showroom where I'd left him.

Hoping my last enchantment had worked, I eased my head around the corner to take a look.

You know, most times, things don't go well for me. I more than half-expected to be yanked into the room by my hair, which would make the second time that night such a thing had happened. Tonight, I'd been shot at, slashed, bitten, chased, blown up, and had my back broken. Typical. But sometimes, even I can catch a break, and I took a few seconds to relish my success.

The spell I'd added to the disco lightshow had worked perfectly. I'd modified the bright flashes and incessant screeching noises and slowly morphed them into something mesmerizing and hypnotic instead. Soothing, even. When he'd calmed enough, I'd sent him elsewhere again, but this time, I'd pulled out all the stops. Max ended up on a tropical beach, where the warm breezes caressed him, and the sounds of the ocean waves had worked their own magick. I mean, he was *there*. It took a lot out of me, especially after that grenade, but seeing Max on the floor with his head pillowed on one muscular arm made me sigh with relief. I'd calmed the savage beast and put his ass to sleep. In slumber, he reverted to human form, just as I hoped he would. I'd taken a big chance, hoping that I could keep Malleus from pressing his attack on Max, but it had paid off.

I dropped the veil and donned my usual human appearance as I knelt beside him. It didn't take much prodding to wake him up, though I admit I poked him a couple of times and stepped well back. You know...just in case. He stirred, opened his eyes, and focused them on me. I raised my hands in a calming gesture.

"Hey," I kept my voice low. *Let's not startle the werewolf.* "It's all right. It's me. Kane. Malleus took over Ariana's body, and he's locked himself in an office over there. You okay?"

144

Max sat up, completely unconcerned about his nudity. He seemed somewhat bewildered, but awareness rapidly dawned in his eyes. He absently flexed the fingers of his right hand, then shook them out a little, as if dismissing a trifling ache. I swear, I'd nearly broken that finger off a few minutes before, but he healed almost as quickly as I do.

"I. . ." he stammered at first, but gained confidence as his senses came online, "Yes, I believe I am. Did I hear you correctly? Malleus is in Ariana's body?"

I nodded. "Yep. It sucks."

"How in the blue hell did that happen?"

I shrugged my shoulders. "Occupational hazard. He was tracking our progress through an energy link in the cuffs. She cut off the link, there was an accident of some kind and they switched bodies. We didn't know until it was too late. Gotta get him out of there."

"I couldn't agree more." Max shook his head. "The last thing I remember clearly is her coming to me, then you burst through the window and tackled us both." He paused a moment, thinking. "Wait, she threw a spell at me! I was about to ask you what was going on, and I saw her face." A dangerous frown appeared, "That makes perfect sense, then. That expression of hatred, that wasn't her face at all. After she cast whatever that was, all I could think of was killing you. He caught me with my defenses down." He offered me a rueful smile. "Terribly sorry about that."

"Not your fault," I assured him. "I'm of half a mind to send you out of here. He wants you dead, either by my hand or his own. I can't let him escape, but we can't rough up Ariana's body too much, either."

He laughed, "I'm not going anywhere until we finish this." He became serious once more, "Ariana. Where is she? Her spirit?" I heard the concern in his voice.

"She's imprisoned in Malleus's body. She can't move or talk like Malleus can. I left her with Detective Avery, so she's safe. She went to get Cyrus. He might be able to switch them back." *If he's still alive,* I thought.

"So, we've got to subdue Malleus without hurting Ariana's body. Capture him." Max's gears were turning the same way mine had. "Get them switched back without getting ourselves killed." He glanced down at the bone cuffs. "And get those damned things off of your wrists."

"You've got it."

"How long do we have before they do their work?"

"Less than an hour, I'd say."

A decidedly wolfish grin appeared on Max's handsome face. He rolled his impressive shoulders back and cracked his neck. Standing at his full height, he towered over me, a graceful and ferocious giant of a man.

"I guess we'd better get to work, then."

That's when we both felt a ponderous thump from somewhere in the deserted store. Something had arrived. Sharp ticking noises followed, like pickaxes striking stone. A feral hiss drifted through the empty store to be answered by others, and we knew that Malleus had not been idle in the last few minutes.

Max took a long, careful step and peered around the jagged opening in the wall, surveying the situation. He seemed to be counting. Then he turned his attention back to me and smiled again.

"If the stakes weren't so high, this might be fun."

He flexed his arms a little and bowed his head, and I felt a pulse of energy from within him. When he raised his head again, his eyes had gone all amber-gold, and his smile had widened. Fur sprouted as he shifted back into the ferocious being that had pursued me for the better part of the evening. Seconds later, he looked down at me, fully seven feet of smiling humanoid wolf. Standing still and up close, he was even more impressive, all muscle

146

and quickness. He threw back his head and howled, powerful and eager to fight whatever Malleus threw our way. Then he turned and plowed right through the wall in a burst of chalky sheetrock dust as he flung himself into the fray.

Max is definitely a creature after my own heart, I thought. *I like this guy.*

I veiled myself and followed through the opening, looking forward to fighting alongside him instead of against him.

Chapter 16

I've fought hundreds of different demons in my time. They came in a wide variety of shapes and sizes, equipped with an equally wide variety of weapons, though size and pure muscle were often the issue. This time, I had to tip my hat to Malleus for calling up something a bit more interesting for us to deal with.

Three demons stared at us from the other side of the store. They stood about as tall as I, but twitchy and quick. Ordinarily, three of anything smaller than a fully grown hill giant wouldn't bother me. But these things were...wow, they were sharp *everywhere*. Metallic-looking scales resembling tiny shingles made of razor blades covered their bodies. Huge bulbous eyes glowed pale green, the same sickly color as the energy Malleus manifested before, and lipless slashes skinned away from rows of pointed teeth any shark would envy.

Slender-waisted, the creatures boasted powerful muscles in their chests, shoulders, and thighs. Their arms hung far nearly to the ground, covered with ropes of wiry muscle. Their hands ended in claws that looked more like blades than an animal's talons. Their legs bent backwards at the knees, and the ticking sounds we'd heard came from their feet. Well, they didn't have feet, exactly. Below the knee, each leg ended in a shining spike of bone that speared the tile floor with every step they took. One kick or slash from those things could skewer or disembowel an enemy.

To make matters worse, ropy tentacles sprouted from the creature's backs. They waved in the air like cobras looking for prey. They, too, were armored in sharp scales, and tipped with a wicked-looking hook of bone. As I watched, one whipped out at least three times the distance I'd have though it could possibly reach before snapping back. The demons hissed again, twitching their heads in all directions, oddly birdlike as they talked among themselves.

I'll say this for him, Max didn't mess around. He grabbed an entire section of empty shelves and threw it across the room. It hit the rightmost demon squarely and smashed it into the wall of the office. The impact took all the fight out of it, and its misshapen head lolled to one side as it either died or lost consciousness.

One down, two to go, I thought, looking over the two remaining creatures. Their armor didn't expose much for me to slash. Even their necks were covered. I needed to be creative. Max circled around to our right, aiming to get the creatures in a line so they couldn't both attack him at once, so I went the opposite direction. The demon on that side regarded me with a dull green stare, ignoring its remaining partner and Max. Its glowing eyes tracked my every move as I circled to my left. *So much for using my veils. It can see me. Geez, can everyone see me?*

I exploded forward, intent on slashing the demon's head right off its shoulders. Of course, it protested. Its hook-barbed tentacles snapped through the air towards me, forcing me to gyrate and twist hard enough that I thought my spine was going to snap. Again. I dodged, ducked, and wove my way towards it. I evaded the worst of its attack, but still took a couple of lashes across my back and left shoulder as its tentacles thrashed around me. That hurt. And it pissed me off.

I darted inside the reach of its overlong arms and tried to open him up with my claws, but they skated off his scales, leaving little more than rows of thick scratches on their chitinous surface. It screeched and grabbed me in a bear hug, pinning my arms to my sides. Every point of contact with its scales left stinging cuts and gashes. I'd be slashed to ribbons if I stayed much longer, but its grip was ferociously strong. The pressure increased, squeezing the breath out of me, and I knew I'd better improvise.

The best I could do was slam my forehead into its face, so I did. Repeatedly. Bones crunched under my assault, and the thing screeched in pain. Its grip loosened and it wobbled, momentarily stunned. I took advantage of its moment of weakness and shrugged off its grasping arms. I reached up and gripped its head and jaw in my clawed hands and twisted sharply, using every bit of my strength.

The crack as its neck broke was deeply satisfying, I have to tell you. It hissed as it went down, the deflated wheeze of a dying creature. It fell to the floor in a tangle of limbs and tentacles.

Max roared in fury nearby and I looked up to see him locked in combat with the remaining beast. He grappled with it, and the whole affair looked painful. Each had one wrist clamped in a ferocious grip so neither could really gain advantage over the other, but the demon's tentacles were everywhere. They whipped, slashed, and cut at Max's broad back and arms, leaving bloody lines of scarlet everywhere they touched. To make things worse, it repeatedly stabbed it's pointed legbones down and into Max's feet, piercing them when he didn't yank them away fast enough. The brawl resembled a mad ballroom dance, though I'd seldom seen one so bloody. They moved around the room, struggling to gain advantage as they strained within each other's grip for a few seconds more, then Max came to a similar conclusion as mine.

He reached out and bit the thing's head off.

Yep. Just opened his mouth wide and closed his enormous jaws over the creature's scaly noggin. It looked surprised in the instant I could still see its face. Then Max crunched his jaws shut and gave a couple of ferocious yanks with his powerful neck muscles. That was all she wrote. Its head came off with a hideous squelching sound, leaving the body flailing about as it tried to interpret the sudden lack of signals from its brain. It dropped to its knees and fell over sideways as Max spat the loathsome head off to one side, then spat again and shook his own head in disgust. *Must have tasted awful,* I thought. Max heaved a few deep breaths and wavered a bit on his feet before righting himself. He was bleeding from a score of wounds, some looking downright severe, but other than the moment of exhaustion I'd just seen, he bore the pain stoically. He shook his head again, then squared his shoulders as he fought off the fatigue that crept in around the edges.

We both looked at the third demon, but Max's shelf-heaving attack had killed it right off. It was already dissolving in black, silent flames that left no trace of it against the shattered wall. The others would disappear the same way before long.

That left Malleus. We were now on the better end of two against one. Max growled low in his throat, and his eyes darted to the office where Malleus had hidden. He glanced at me, then nodded towards the door. Together, we approached the office, wary of any signs Malleus was brewing up another demonic summoning. All was silent.

"Malleus!" Max's voice startled me, low and rumbling as boulders crashing together. Few werewolves I'd ever known had been able to speak while in wolf form, but as I'd repeatedly seen, Max wasn't an ordinary werewolf. "Who are you? What do you want of me?"

Silence fell as we waited for an answer. Several seconds ticked by before Malleus replied from within the office, his voice cold and clear. "Your death, Maximus. Your just punishment for past misdeeds."

"What misdeeds?" If a werewolf's growling voice could ever be called sympathetic, Max somehow managed it just then. "If I've wronged you, I've no knowledge of it.

There's no need to make others suffer because of me. Tell me what I can do to make this right."

I shook my head. I'd rather just tear the guy's head off, but that wouldn't help Ariana in the least. Nor would it help me keep my hands. I gritted my teeth and waited to see how things would play out. Maybe Max could pull off a miracle here. A stupid flicker of hope had the gall to appear in my heart, dumb as that was.

There was no response for a long moment, then the office door opened. The gun barrel emerged first, at the end of Ariana's steady arm. Malleus had screwed her pretty face into a narrow-eyed expression of absolute hatred; it was practically coming off him in waves. He saw me first and motioned me backwards with the gun barrel. I obliged by taking a single step back to give him space. His eyes fell on Max, and the hate I felt from him intensified.

"You!" Ariana's mouth said the word, but the hint of a southern accent betrayed Malleus's emotion. Several seconds passed as he stared at Max, the object of his obsession. His words came out in a hissing whisper, "Your company bought ours. Remember? Mallinson's Manufacturing. Thirty years ago, you rolled over us like a juggernaught."

Max's canine face was still supremely expressive, and I saw him frown as he considered this information.

"Georgia?" he ventured.

"Yes!" Ariana's eyes went wide as Malleus affirmed Max's memory, and her body shook with barely suppressed rage. "Yes, that's it! You bought us out and then fired him! Him! It was *his* company, damn you!"

Max's enormous hands slowly rose before him in a ca ming gesture, though I'm sure the claws he sported negated the calming effect. Even so, he was trying.

"One of my regional managers oversaw that takeover. If he did something wrong, I'll make him answer

152

for it. Even so, I take responsibility for his actions," he glanced at me, "Release my friend from your bargain. I'll deal with you personally, Malleus. I'll make this right."

Ariana barked with harsh, shaky laughter, "Oh, you'll make it right, will you? Throw money at me to shut me up? I'm afraid that won't work, Maximus. He's dead. He lost his mind after he lost his business." Ariana's eyes went wide as the words came out, shining with madness.

Shit, I thought. *Looks like Malleus's daddy wasn't the only one who's gone around the bend.*

"He didn't die right away, either. No, it took him a couple of years. At first, he was just quiet. He took to spending time in the basement. But then he started taking us down there. In the dark. There were four of us. My mother, my sister, and me." His gaze took on a faraway look and his voice trembled. "I hid from him one day. I didn't want to go down there again. They all went down with him, though. And they never came up. None of them."

Max stayed still as a statue, listening intently. I think he might have thought he still had a chance to talk Malleus out of the tree. But I knew better. He wasn't coming out of the crazy tree until I climbed up there and knocked him out of it. He was insane.

Ariana's big blue eyes came back into focus and narrowed at Max. "All because of *you*. And now you'll pay for it." Malleus turned and pointed the gun at me. "You know what's going to happen if you don't honor your word, GrimFaerie. Last time I checked, the deadline isn't far away. The only hope you have of keeping your hands and your magick is to kill him. Right now." I said nothing. Which infuriated him. "Do it!" he spat.

In my mind's eye, I saw Malleus's ugly spirit rather than the body it occupied. I dropped my gaze down to my hands, cast a quick glance at Max, then eyed the sorcerer once more. A grin of triumph appeared at one side of

Ariana's mouth, threatening to turn into a full-blown smile. He thought he'd won. That did it. I'd had enough of his arrogant bullshit.

"Up yours, Malleus. I don't need hands to deal with the likes of you. I'll just rip your throat out with my teeth. You'll be just as dead."

Astonishment dawned on Ariana's face as Malleus digested the words. And he paused to consider them for a hair too long.

I'd recovered more than well enough to dart forward and yank the gun from Ariana's grip. I tried to do it without damaging anything, but Malleus screamed anyway, and then I punched him right in Ariana's face, putting just enough force into the blow that I'd surely knock him out without breaking Ariana's neck.

The shockwave was instantaneous, and I admit, a surprise. As my fist was supposed to be knocking Malleus unconscious, it instead triggered whatever defense mechanism he'd cast upon himself, and the result was impressive. The blast of greenish power went off like a bomb, throwing both me and Max away from Malleus to tumble through the air and into the showroom we'd just vacated, demolishing the rest of the wall on the way. I lay there, stunned, and not a little pissed that I'd been suckered.

Ariana's voice, still tinted with crazy, taunted us from across the store. "Seriously, Grim, you think I don't know how fast you are? You think I'd depend solely on the gun to protect myself? This body has its limitations, but I'm still more than powerful enough to deal with you if you keep insisting on avoiding your bargain! Just kill him and be done with it!"

I tried to respond with my usual wit, but I had nothing. Wow, I hurt. To be honest it had been a long night, and that blast was far worse than the flashbang. That had been a purely physical explosion, while this thing had hit me on a magickal level. I felt like a worn-out rag doll right about then. I searched for Max only to find him face down in an awkward position, unmoving. I didn't think anything was broken, but for the moment, he was out, and even as I watched, he began to shift back to his human form.

Uh, oh, I thought. I don't like when I think that. It means things are bad. And by any definition, the situation was definitely not good. Far from it. I tried to move and found that my muscles had gone on strike, courtesy of Malleus's whammy. In a rare display of self-indulgent pessimism, I thought it again. Uh, oh. This really sucks.

I raised my head and saw that Ariana now glowed with power, emitting an energy so intense that it looked almost solid, an aura that extended at least two feet beyond her physical form. As I watched, the glow began to coalesce, resolving itself into a human shape around her, solidifying until her body disappeared from view inside it. The head took on a masculine appearance, eyes, nose, and mouth, all forming before my eyes until I recognized the features of the body we'd found earlier.

Malleus, I thought.

The sorcerous construct grew more solid by the moment. Its feet pressed into the floor as it gained mass, and I heard the floor tiles beneath its feet crack and shift as they accepted its ponderous weight. The creature raised one hand in front of its face, examining its fingers in wonder. It made a fist that looked about the size of a bowling ball and just as dangerous. Its glowing green eyes fastened on me on the floor, several yards away. It grinned and spoke in a powerful, booming voice that had barely a hint of Ariana's within it. "You're useless, GrimFaerie! The fabled assassin, bah! Worthless! Never mind, I'll just kill you both myself!"

The energy-being burst forward, bloodlust plain on its green face. It had become solid and heavy enough that its feet cracked the floor as it ran, and I figured he'd just pummel us to death with his oversized green fists. Death by Hulk smash. I struggled to move into something resembling a defensive stance, but not much happened. I didn't even make it into a sitting position. Rage boiled through me, but even that hot-burning fuel did little but make me snarl at Malleus. I knew I'd end up dying at some point, but wow, this was embarrassing. I pushed myself up on one elbow, determined to meet my death as vertical as possible.

That's when things got interesting. In my line of work, that's saying something.

Chapter 17

Malleus broke into a full-on sprint in our direction, intent on ushering us into the next plane of existence. He looked pretty optimistic about his chances, too. At least he did, until a silvery web of energy flew out of the back of the store, snaring him. The glowing net hit him hard, knocking him off his feet as it swirled around him and clamped his arms and legs together. He bellowed in rage and surprise as he hit the floor, struggling against the trap. He strained mightily for a couple of seconds before he burst free of the snare, disintegrating it in a flash of argent light. He sat up with a howl of anger and turned his attention to the loading dock. A figure stepped out from behind the shelves, and my spirits lifted. Old Cyrus had come to play.

"Malleus, you shiite! Back off, ya walloper!" Cyrus held a crystal sphere in his right hand like a shot put, and it glowed with the same silvery power that had fueled the mystical net. I smiled. Cyrus had been around a long time. He knew some things, and he wasn't being taken by surprise this time. "You're fooling around with arts that are beyond you! Let the girl go and stop this foolishness before you hurt yourself!" He lifted his left hand and it, too, took on a clean, bright glow of energy.

Malleus got to his feet and looked down at the wizened old sorcerer across the room. He laughed. "Seriously? You think you can beat me in a contest of skills? I'll have you know—"

Cyrus blasted him in the face with a focused, intense bolt of power about four inches wide. It slammed into Malleus's big green forehead, rocking his head back and cutting off his commentary. Before he could recover, Cyrus hit him again, and a third time, driving Malleus down to one knee as he clutched his face. Becoming a being of solid energy had its good points but being solid also meant he could be hit. And from the expression on his face, it looked like it hurt.

"Ye talk too much, ya wee radge!" Cyrus threw a jagged bolt of silver lighting across the room, but this time, Malleus deflected it and threw one of his own. Cyrus ducked behind the shelves, which exploded. The game was on.

I managed to sit up, my healing powers doing their damned job. Nothing felt broken this time, at least. I was still too weak to do much, but given a couple minutes, I'd happily rip Malleus's giant green head off his neck. Max groaned nearby and also sat up.

"It's been a long while since I've been hit like that," Max sighed, rubbing one hand over his face. "What's going on?"

"Cyrus is here. He's fighting Malleus." I explained the obvious as Malleus roared in fury and stomped towards the maze of shelves where Cyrus had taken refuge, while the old man tossed a few more bolts of energy at him, forcing Malleus to duck and dodge.

"Ah, good. Cyrus is quite capable." Max looked over at the hulking green form Malleus had taken and his eyebrows rose in surprise. "That's new."

"Yeah, it's solid and strong. Not sure how he pulled that off. Ariana's body is inside there, but I think that hitting the energy form won't hurt her physically. Hurts Malleus, though."

Max frowned and looked at me as he pushed himself to his feet. He shifted back into his wolf form and rumbled, "Are you sure? We're not going to hurt her?"

I wanted to say yes. I really did. But the best I could do was, "I think so. Just aim for the head. It's at least a foot away from where hers is inside there, and it looks to be a viable target."

There was an enormous whump of power, and Malleus's green body flew past us. It impacted the far wall with a crash then slumped to the floor. He wasn't unconscious, though. Just mad.

"Lucky shot!" Malleus yelled.

"Yer bum's out the windae!" Cyrus shot back, "You're outclassed! Give it up!"

"Outclassed, am I?" A wicked grin appeared on Malleus's face as he came to his feet.

Uh oh, I thought. Pissing contests between wizards are often dangerous. And we were ringside.

Malleus raised both hands, a wild grin on his face. "We'll see about that." His hands glowed, and Max and I tensed, preparing for some huge eruption of power. Our eyes darted to Cyrus, who had emerged from the shelves again, still holding the glowing silver crystal. A sparkling shield of energy appeared around him, a protective dome of power. I raised an eyebrow and leveled Cyrus up in my estimation.

The shield didn't help, though. Without warning, Cyrus dropped at least a foot as though he'd fallen through a trap door. He grunted in surprise and flailed his arms to keep his balance, then looked down at his feet.

I looked too, only to discover that they'd vanished. I looked more closely and realized that Malleus had somehow changed the consistency of the floor and foundation beneath Cyrus, momentarily making them both soft enough for the old wizard to sink up to his knees. Of course, he then resolidified everything, entombing Cyrus's legs as if he'd been standing there when the foundation was newly poured. It was a neat trick, an impressive expression of earth magick. Cyrus tried to pull free, but quickly realized that he was trapped and stopped wasting the effort. He scowled at Malleus, silent for the moment as he considered his next move.

"Now, I've got you," Malleus drawled in his syrupy Southern accent. "Just a helpless old man now, aren't you?"

"You'll not succeed here, Malleus! You don't know what you're doing!" Cyrus was pissed, but unafraid. I knew he'd been in worse predicaments, though by human reckoning, it had been a while. He began a chant as he tried to counteract Malleus's trap. It didn't appear to be going well.

Malleus scoffed, "Of course, I know what I'm doing! I'm exacting my revenge and rolling over anyone who gets in my way. You can't stop me! The werewolf can't stop me, and neither can the vaunted GrimFaerie!"

I was about to take exception to that remark. I'd had far more of Malleus's bullshit than I could take, and since I was about to lose my hands anyway, I figured I'd better use my claws on him as soon as possible. I took a step out of the showroom and prepared to fling myself at him. But then a feminine voice echoed in the empty space, hard but beautiful.

"They might not. But maybe I can."

Detective Avery Lynne stepped from the shadows off to Malleus's left, her face set with determination and anger. The instant she came into view, I felt her power rising, vibrating the air around her. Its intense hum permeated me, energized me. My eyes widened as I took in her stance, felt her intensity. A hot, blue-green glow seeped from her skin as she gathered her energy, and she looked every inch a warrior-mage.

Oh man, she was *gorgeous*.

Malleus shifted his attention to her, and he started in surprise. He smirked and raised his left hand to loose a huge bolt of green energy, intending to blast her out of her shoes.

She raised her left arm in a defensive motion, and I noticed that she had something attached to her forearm.

160

A shield! A small metal oval was strapped there, a buckler, most likely courtesy of Cyrus. I wouldn't have thought she'd know how to use such a thing, but she leaned into the oncoming blast like a Spartan. She fed energy into the artifact on her arm, and it glowed brightly in response. The killer blast slammed into her shield and neatly parted to either side, leaving Avery untouched, but tearing up everything from floor to ceiling around and behind her.

Avery lowered the shield, and one side of her mouth turned up in a smug little grin.

"My turn, hotshot."

I thought she'd pull a gun, but she surprised me yet again by producing a slender wooden rod about as thick as her thumb, inscribed with glowing ancient runes. It flared like a blue sun and the blast of magickfire she sent at Malleus made Cyrus's previous attack look puny. A bolt of white-hot energy about as thick as my thigh slammed into Malleus's head, taking him off his feet with gusto. He flopped to the floor with an earth-shaking thump, stunned by the pure power of her attack.

Avery staggered and went down to a knee. The unaccustomed sensation of fear blossomed in me for a moment, and I left Max, sprinting across the room to her side. I grabbed her arm to steady her. She was exhausted.

"You hurt?" I asked, thinking that fewer words might hide all the ridiculous feelings I'd been having lately. I don't think it worked.

Avery used my arm to pull herself to her feet. She shook her head. "Don't get all mushy on me, lover boy. That took a lot out of me. I'm new at this." Her tone went all business again as switched to her cop voice. Her warrior voice. "Get this on Malleus! Hurry, before he recovers!" She handed me the end of a copper chain, thick enough to be strong without being heavy. An

161

unlocked padlock was threaded through the final link. "Just get it wrapped around him and lock it shut! Do it now!"

I don't like taking orders from humans, even hot ones. But Avery seemed to have something up her sleeve, and far be it from me to argue when I could be messing with the bad guy. I bolted for him, trailing the chain behind me. Whatever she'd hit him with, it must have hurt, because Malleus had just managed to sit back up, and the expression on his emerald face showed nothing but agony. I whipped the chain around his body twice and clicked the lock into place. I should have been clawing at his exposed neck. The heartbeat of time it took me to lock the chain loop closed was more than enough for him to decide to hit me.

And hit me, he did. He put everything he had into it, and that was a lot. I flew through the air, stunned enough that I didn't really care what I landed on. Floor, office wall, shelves, whatever. I'd find out soon enough.

I landed awkwardly and upside down in a solid pair of furry arms. My face was mashed into something. . .odd. That's when I realized that Max had caught me. Awkward. He turned me right side up and put me back on my feet as quickly as he could. We both pretended it didn't happen.

Meanwhile, Malleus had made it to his feet, mumbling in fury. He touched the chain wrapped around his body and I could see the confusion on his face, but I knew it wouldn't last long. We didn't have much time, but Avery wasn't waiting on us anyway.

"Cyrus! Do it now! They're linked!"

I glanced at her and saw her holding the chain over her head in both hands. The end she'd given me was seconds away from becoming a real problem, as Malleus was reaching for the chain with both of his enormous hands. I followed the line of the chain to the opposite end and saw that it was attached to one side of a pair of handcuffs. The other cuff was attached to the wrist of a body that I hadn't yet seen, hidden off to Avery's side as it was. Malleus's physical body had been duct taped to a big orange moving dolly and leaned against a nearby wall. His head lolled forward in unconsciousness, and I noted that it was a less handsome version of the green monstrosity that currently housed Ariana's body. Malleus's construct stood and grabbed the chains, preparing to do something extremely unhelpful.

Cyrus wasted no time. He yelled a handful of arcane syllables and threw a jagged, silvery bolt of energy across the room, slow motion lightning that drove away what remained of the room's shadows. It hit the chain between Avery's hands and turned it into a glowing serpent of light. Avery gritted her teeth and grunted as she added her own prodigious power to the chain, intensifying its glow enough that I had to shield my eyes.

Malleus screamed as Cyrus's energy flowed from the chain into his body-construct, burning him from the inside out. On the other end of the chain, Malleus's physical body likewise shone with blue-white light. He screamed again, a cry of anger and frustration, as well as pain, and the light grew brighter, and brighter still as the spell took hold. I crouched down, knowing what would come next, and Max followed my lead.

The spell did its work, and a shockwave exploded outwards from the chain, sweeping across the dusty floor and rattling the entire building. The light spell Malleus cast earlier blew apart, leaving the place in darkness, and silence fell. All was still.

I leapt to my feet. "Avery!" She'd fallen, and was still lying on the floor, unmoving. I raced to her side and knelt down to cradle her head in my arms. She was still breathing, but that was about all I could tell. "Avery! Are you all right?" Silence was her only response. My heart ached and my throat locked up.

Her eyelids fluttered open and she gasped, heaving in a big, startled breath. Her eyes focused on mine. "Uh," she began. She appeared to examine and discard several phrases before settling on, "Did it work?"

I searched for Malleus's green creation, but it was gone. Lying on the floor in its place was Ariana's slim form, silent and still. I turned back to Avery, her head still in my lap. "I think so. Let me check on her." I meant to get right up. I did. But holding her head in my hands like that, looking down at those grey-green-blue eyes, I must have paused for just long enough. Avery smiled and blushed, and I made myself look away. "Be right back," I added, just to say something.

I got up and left Avery to fend for herself as I hustled over to Ariana. She looked awfully small lying there, her blond hair spread out on the floor beneath her, her arms and legs awkwardly bent and still. I've seen a lot of corpses and they often looked like that. Exactly like that, in fact. Steeling myself for whatever might come, I gently touched my fingers to her neck. Her pulse was strong, steady, and slow as ever. I reached into her mind and promptly ran into her usual automatic defenses. *Yep,* I thought, *she's back. It's definitely her in there.* I sighed in relief. I leaned close so she'd hear me.

"Hey. Loser. You're missing the fun stuff. Wake up." I slapped her face on either side until she started flinching and then her eyes popped open and she gasped.

"Kane!" Ariana sat up. "What happened? Am I. . .?" She gave herself a quick patdown and sighed, "Whew! Sweet baby monkeys, that was awful! Oh, ow, what the hell is wrong with my foot? Dammit, that hurts!" She reached for her foot, her face echoing the pain she felt there. Her gaze fell on the chain that loosely wrapped around her. She followed it with her eyes to Avery, and beyond the detective to the duct-taped body secured at the other end of the chain. His head hung down on his chest, still unconscious. Her eyes narrowed in anger. "You. Son. Of. A. *Bitch!*" Ariana jumped up to her feet, letting the chain drop to the floor around her, and she limped towards Malleus, grunting in pain with every step. I figured she was going to do something awful to him. I could hardly wait. She grabbed a fistful of his hair, picked his head up so she could aim better, and drew back a fist to knock him even further unconscious. Just as Malleus blearily opened one eye, I remembered the last time I'd tried that, when he was in Ariana's body. It hadn't ended well for me. He was back in his own body now, with full access to his own powers.

Shit.

"Ariana, wait!" I yelled, but even as the words left my mouth, she punched Malleus for all she was worth. He grinned as her fist whizzed through the air.

The blast was bigger than last time. It threw us all away from him, tumbling as though we'd been shot out of a cannon. I was ready this time, though. I twisted my body and managed to land on my hands and feet, and I dug my claws into the floor so I'd stay put. I looked over to see that Max had done pretty much the same thing, though he was shaking his head a bit, disoriented. Avery and Ariana fared worse, but they managed to somewhat break their falls when they landed. They lay where they fell, out of the fight. I hoped they weren't too badly hurt.

"Time's running out, GrimFaerie!" Malleus yelled, finally using his own voice instead of Ariana's. A quick blast of green fire split the duct tape wide open and he walked free of the dolly as though that had been his plan all along. His cloak was thrown back and he strutted towards us to stand, hands on hips, a malevolent grin on his rugged face. Wow, I hated him. He raised both hands, wreathing them with bright emerald fire, and proceeded to taunt me. "You've got maybe two minutes before my cuffs do their work. Are you going to fulfill the bargain, or do I just kill all of you myself?"

As if to emphasize his words, both cuffs tightened on my wrists, cutting into the skin. It hurt, and I knew it would only get worse. I growled in frustration and clenched my fists through the pain. My time was almost up.

That's when I got an idea. Or was it a gift from the Goddess? I cut my eyes over to Max, who'd regained his senses and was staring daggers at Malleus. I rolled the idea over in my mind. It was distasteful. And risky. If it didn't work, there'd be hell to pay. But I'd be in worse shape if I didn't try it.

"*Max.*" I got his attention, and his ferocious glare landed on me. Didn't scare me a bit, nope. "Max, do you trust me?"

Have you ever seen a werewolf look surprised? Me either. Well, until that moment, anyway. Now, I had. He stared at me with those golden-amber eyes, and he nodded.

"Lose the wolf."

Max blinked at me, glanced over at Malleus, then focused on me again as he thought that over. He closed his eyes and took about five seconds to return to his human form.

"What have you got in mind?"

I told him. He didn't like it, not one bit. In fact, he stared at me like I'd gone completely insane. Maybe I had, but I'd run out of time and options.

"There's no other way?"

I shook my head. "If I could think of one, I wouldn't ask this of you."

He looked down at my hands and saw the blood. It dripped to the floor in a steady patter. When his eyes returned to mine, I knew that he'd made his decision.

"If this goes badly, promise me that you'll make him pay for it. And that you'll watch over Ariana."

I nodded. "I'll bring Malleus down right now or die trying."

"Well enough, then. Do it."

Max dropped to both knees on the floor, closed his eyes, and lifted his chin. I moved around behind him, wrapped my arm around his neck and secured what I'd heard Ariana and Avery call a rear-naked choke. Using every bit of my Fae strength, I squeezed for all I was worth.

Max stayed still for a moment, accepting his fate. As the blood flow to his brain ceased and his vision began to narrow, he reflexively reached up and grabbed my arm to steady himself, but he didn't try to escape. I knew he could if he wanted to, and so did he. But he didn't struggle. He was letting me strangle the life out of him. Gradually, his movements slowed, then finally stopped as his consciousness fled. If I let go now, the blood would slam back into his head and he'd just wake right up, so I held fast. The thump of his heart had reached triphammer levels, but it was slowing. Somewhere at the periphery of my awareness, I could hear Malleus's laughter. I gritted my teeth and tried to shut it out.

"Kane, no!" Ariana yelled. She'd regained her feet and was hobbling painfully towards us. Avery was a couple of steps behind. They were both wide-eyed with horror. "What are you doing? Let him go!"

I ignored them. I only needed to hold him a little longer. Ariana plowed into us both, knocking us down, frantically pulling at my arms. I held on. She started slapping me, screaming, crying, desperately trying to get me off of Max. I protected my face as best I could, finishing the stranglehold with all my strength. Avery stood by, shocked and confused. Her wand glowed fiercely at her side, but she didn't use it on me. I heard her voice

167

mingled with Ariana's as she, too, implored me to let him go.

I wouldn't. I couldn't. It had to be this way.

Max's body collapsed against me, limp and unmoving. Moments later, his once thunderous heartbeat faded until I couldn't hear it anymore. Even so, I held on. Malleus's laughter echoed throughout the building, mingling with Ariana's angry cries and Avery's raised voice. I shut it all out.

By my hand, Maximus Lucanis von Gerhardt died that night. I killed him. It's what I do.

True to the bargain that was made with my blood, the cuffs cracked open and fell off my wrists. I looked across the floor at Malleus, still laughing, still thinking he'd won.

I released Max and gave Ariana a quick and well-timed shove. Caught off guard, she slipped and fell on her butt, which gave me some room to move. I laid Max's body carefully down on the floor and turned back to Ariana before she launched herself at me again.

"Listen!" I bellowed. "He agreed to this! Do that CPR thing and get him back! Do you understand?"

Her eyes widened and I saw comprehension fighting its way through her emotions. "He what? Wait—CPR?"

Avery caught on right away. She stepped over to Max and knelt beside him, clasping her hands over his sternum with both her palms facing down. She started chest compressions in sharp, measured movements and I could hear her counting under her breath. She took a moment to direct Ariana, "Breathe for him. Tilt his head back, pinch his nose shut, and cover your mouth with his. Two breaths for every 30 of my compressions. Do it!"

Ariana looked from her to me and set her mouth in a grim line as she nodded. An instant later, she was on her knees next to Max, doing as she'd been directed.

Avery looked up at me with her storm-green eyes. "You go get that son of a bitch. We've got this."

I got to my feet and looked across the empty store at Malleus. He had an enormous grin on his face. "I told you! I told you you'd do my bidding, GrimFaerie! And now he's dead! Ha!"

Cyrus's voice cut through my angry thoughts, "Kane!" I whipped my head in his direction. "Here! Catch!" He pulled something out of a pocket and tossed it to me. It glittered in the air, all silver and sparkle, and I caught it in one hand. I opened my fingers to see a small crystal sphere the size of a marble worked into a silver setting that hung at the end of a silver chain. I glanced up at Cyrus. "It's a ward crystal! It'll help repel his force attacks! Just put it on!"

I slipped the chain over my head and its power vibrated through me. If it worked at all, it would at least give me an edge. I extended my claws and cracked my neck in each direction. Playtime had arrived. I turned around.

"Hey," I said, giving Malleus my full, unwavering attention. He stopped laughing. I dropped my disguise so he could see me, my true self. I wasn't as big as the demons he'd summoned, and not as physically imposing as Max. But I'm a GrimFaerie, gods damn it.

I've traveled this earth for centuries, killing everything that's gotten in my way. Demons, trolls, monsters, and men, I've slain them all. I've taken down beings whose power made Malleus look like a mewling child. I've walked the edge between life and death countless times without fear, and I've sent hundreds of evil warlocks and wizards screaming into the abyss, wailing for mercy they'd never receive. I had no fear. Only rage. And I let it all out, projecting my feelings across that empty space so Malleus would know exactly what kind of trouble he was in. He was warded against a lot of things, I was certain. But I'm a GrimFaerie. It was time for him to fear me.

Shock appeared on his face as my sending took hold in him. His sharp arrogance drained away and he suddenly seemed to realize he'd made a mistake, a very bad one. I'd done his job, all right, but I was still alive. And free to do as I wished. I roared a wordless challenge, and he flinched. He brought up his hands, still wreathed in a green glow of malevolent power. I just smiled.

"Let's go, asshole."

Chapter 18

Malleus regained his composure pretty quickly. He began chanting in Latin and his hands grew brighter as he gathered power to throw at me.

I started towards him, slowly at first, then I picked up speed. I wanted him to see me. When I'd crossed half the space between us, I cast a veil over myself, rendering my body invisible. Thus hidden, I leapt, reaching for the exposed ceiling joists above me, muting the noise I made when I got there. My initial plan was to monkey across the joists then drop down on top of him. I'd momentarily forgotten that he'd seen through that enchantment back in the stadium.

A blast of emerald power hit me, rocking me and dislodging my grip from the slender steel support I'd been holding. As I fell, I twisted my body in the air so that I'd end up on my feet. When I landed, I realized a couple of things at once: First, the crystal Cyrus gave me worked quite well. I'd felt the impact of Malleus's blast, but it barely hurt. Second, it occurred to me that discerning a body hidden beneath a veil was a particular skill. It might have a weakness I could exploit. That gave me an idea. I looked up at Malleus only to find him gloating again.

"I told you, I can see you, GrimFaerie!" He jeered. "Your usual hide and seek tactics are useless against me." He pointed a finger at me and loosed another blast, which I neatly sidestepped. "I can do this all day. You can't hide from me!"

"Can't hide, eh?" I dropped the veil and stood my ground, making sure he got another good look at me. "You're absolutely right. I guess I'll have to try something else, then. I'm glad I brought a few friends."

A questioning look appeared on his face, and I knew I had him. It took me a few seconds to focus my will. Hiding myself was easy. This next bit wasn't. It was going to take some major mojo and concentration, but I knew I had it in me. Closing my eyes, I dug deep into my well of magick, deeper than I had in a very long time. I was tired, but I pushed my fatigue aside and focused on one last, Herculean effort, and my power answered my call as I knew it would. I used my will to shape the spell, crafting it to reproduce what I saw in my mind's eye. It took a few important seconds, but Malleus was dumb enough to give them to me, and those few heartbeats of time were enough. I made sure everything was in place in the theater of my mind, then I released all that pent-up energy into the world, guiding it to fulfill its purpose. I heard Malleus gasp. When I opened my eyes and saw what I'd wrought, I couldn't help but bare my fangs in a grin.

Where I'd previously stood alone facing Malleus, now over a hundred GrimFaeries fell in ranks all around me. We were all me, but some had clothing, others were naked. A few even wore armor and bore weapons. Some had long hair like me, others were shaved bald, while still others had their hair braided tightly to their heads with bits of bone and feathers for decoration. They looked like the savages that they were. That I once was. A hundred GrimFaeries from ages past, all me, but not. Vicious killers, each and every one.

My smile was mirrored in a hundred blue-black faces, revealing gleaming fangs that had rent thousands of throats. All of us flexed our claws. And each acted independently of the other, some glancing at their nearest comrades, nodding and smiling as if acknowledging old friends before glaring back at Malleus with murder in our quicksilver eyes. The growl from our throats came out as a low, loud rumble that I knew Malleus could feel in his bones. To him, these creatures were real. They had substance. And they were going to kill him. A look of terror appeared on his face and I couldn't have been happier.

To his credit, Malleus didn't waste words, but instead began flinging blasts at the nearest of my kin, sending them flying back into their brethren with pain in their faces. Those who fell were ignored by the others, who climbed over their bodies and rushed forward, heedless of the bolts of lashing energy that crashed into them.

The wave advanced and the sorcerer panicked, hurling murderous force at everything that came close. He did well at first, scything down the first few rows of Grim warriors before they came within twenty feet of him. The next row made it to ten feet. Then five. Malleus became even more frantic as they got closer and closer with their vicious fangs and deadly claws.

When it looked like Malleus would be overwhelmed, he resorted to a sharp chant and a gesture that created a glowing dome of green energy around himself, a solid but transparent shield. The Grims slammed up against it, growling and slashing at it with their claws and weapons, venting their rage upon its unyielding surface. He watched them with wide eyes as they glared murderously at him through the barrier. He looked terrified, but eventually squared his shoulders and recaptured some of his previous swagger.

"Ha!" He laughed a little too loudly to be genuine. His voice still shook. "Even with that many, you still couldn't take me! I'm safe!"

The Grims reluctantly stopped attacking the dome, but kept their silvery eyes glued to Malleus within. As one, they all stared him down, letting the weight of their gaze crush him. As if at a signal, they parted to allow me to the front. My feet stopped within inches of the shield. I examined the magickal creation, then nodded slowly. I spoke, keeping my words even and steady, just loud enough to reach him through the hum of his warding spell.

"You're safe. But trapped."

"Wrong!" he jabbed a finger towards me. "Lest you forget, I can just open a rift from inside here. I'll be miles away in moments."

The Grims all growled at him, but I raised a hand to quiet them. "I know you can. But you won't get the chance." I paused, enjoying his confusion. He could have opened the rift and slipped through it right then. He should have. But I had his attention, and all I needed was a moment more. "We're all stuck out here, it's true. But we only needed *one* to get inside."

Malleus took in a breath to cast the rift spell, but it was his last. While he was distracted by all the Grims attacking him from the front, I'd darted around behind him, and he'd cast the protective sphere around us both. I reached one hand over his left shoulder and the other under his right arm, plunged my claws into his abdomen and got a good grip under his rib cage. With one savage motion, I ripped his body apart, roaring in triumph. Blood sprayed across the surface of the energy barrier, sizzling as it made contact, and Malleus got to see his insides hit the floor. He gawked at them as the pain overloaded his nervous system.

Into his ear, I whispered, "That's for hurting my friends, Mal. Tell Elias I'm coming for him, too."

Malleus slowly sank to his knees. His mouth worked feebly, but nothing came out but a bubbling, bloody foam. Finally, he pitched forward, falling on his face in his own entrails. Just to be sure, I rolled him over and ripped his heart out. In the old days, I might have taken a few bites out of it. But I'm civilized now. No, I tossed the meaty lump on the floor next to his wide-eyed corpse. I even wiped my hands and arms clean on his cloak.

The dome of power winked out of existence along with his life, and I was left to stare at a small army of GrimFaeries. I looked them over. They were a pretty good-looking bunch, if I did say so myself. All the other GrimFaeries were illusions, even the spokesman. With a wave of my hand, I dispersed the illusion and they disappeared as though they'd never existed at all. Which they hadn't. Well, that's not true. Each and every one had been me at some point in my long life. Memories, all.

"Kane, help us!" Ariana cried.

I looked up to see a sparkling wall of silver light across the room. Cyrus had taken the liberty of shielding the others while Malleus thought he was blasting my clones. As I watched, the wall dissipated, revealing Avery and Ariana still working on Max.

Uh oh, I thought. I figured they'd have him awake at that point. I sprinted across the room to find Avery still ferociously pumping his chest. Sweat freely ran down her face and arms and she cursed with every other compression. Ariana had tears flowing down her face as she waited for the next chance to breath for Max.

Avery spoke without looking at me, her voice terse and hard. "He's not coming back. We need an ambulance." She paused and her voice hitched a little. "It may be too late."

Ariana stared at me, her cornflower blue eyes reddened from crying. She'd never forgive me for this. Hell, I'd never forgive me for this either. Max let me take his life so I could keep my hands. He trusted me. I growled as my rage tried to muscle in on my reason.

Fortunately, I'm stubborn as hell. And I knew a thing or two.

I knelt and put a hand on both of Avery's and stopped her from pumping. "Stop and listen to me. Both of you!" Avery turned sea green eyes my way. Before I could fall into them, I turned and reached a hand towards

Ariana, who stopped crying and reflexively put hers in mine. I pulled her closer, moved Avery's hands and placed both of Ariana's on Max's chest, then replaced Avery's on top of hers.

"Ariana. You can bring him back. Will it so. With all of your love and hope and joy, call to him. He'll answer, I'm sure of it."

She shook her head, but I saw the hope bring light back to her eyes, but her face fell again. "I don't know if I'm strong enough, Kane."

"I know. But it's got to be you that calls him. He'll hear you." Then I turned to Avery. "And you're going to help. You're stronger. She needs your strength. Use your power. Together, you can bring him back."

Avery's eyes widened as she processed my words. "How? I've never done anything like that."

"Remember how you sent that blast at Malleus? Gather your power the same way, but less. Far less. Just a trickle, and tightly controlled. When Ariana calls him, add your power to her call." I paused and squeezed her hands. "You can do it, Avery." I turned back to Ariana, "And so can you. Do it."

It took a couple of seconds, but then Ariana's face got that look I waited for, that ass-kicking look. She nodded, looked at Max's face, then closed her eyes. Ariana called her power and it rose to answer. It was warm and comforting, and it somehow had hints of sunshine, wildflowers, and blue sky mixed in. She glowed with a pale golden light. I heard when she began to call to Max, and her love for him was evident. It was bright and new, and it burned hotly in her. She adored him, and her affection gave her strength.

"Avery, do it now," I urged the detective.

It took a moment longer for her to engage but wow, just as before, her power was an order of magnitude higher than Ariana's. Maybe several, especially since she was supposed to be keeping it light. Too much would burn Max from the inside out. The blue-green glow rose in her body, but far less than when she'd attacked Malleus. As I watched, the power flowed down her arms to join the golden flow of Ariana's magick as it poured into Max's chest, imploring him to come back.

Max's muscular body brightened as their mingled power filled him, energized him, called to him. He left the dusty floor and floated a few inches above it, held aloft by their combined energy and love.

I heard it when his heart started beating again. Damn thing sounded like a bass drum in there as it finally woke up and started to do its damned job. Three or four beats in and Max's amber-gold eyes popped open. All three of them gasped and he settled back to the ground with a thump. He pushed himself to a sitting position and there was suddenly a lot of crying and hugging.

I walked a few steps away, sat down, and sighed. Sometimes, you get yanked around by your hair and get the crap kicked out of you. But other times, things end up all right. I looked over at Malleus's bloody resting place. His body was still over there, thank goodness. I'd had to kill a few sorcerers more than once, but thankfully, it looked like Malleus was a one and done kind of guy.

Max kissed Ariana rather thoroughly, and Avery pushed herself to her feet, obviously looking to give them the illusion of privacy. She walked around Max's legs to where I was sitting, plopped herself down next to me, and stared over at Malleus's remains.

"That went well," she said, smiling. "Kind of messy, but overall, pretty solid work."

I said nothing for a little while. Strong and silent, that's me.

Avery spoke up again. "I—I heard you. Calling me. I came as fast as I could."

Oh, shit. She'd heard that? It had been instinctive, that call. I wasn't sure I'd even meant for her to hear it. I sighed as I quit lying to myself and admitted that I had. I'd wanted nothing in life more than to have her near me.

Finally, I said, "Great." Eloquent as ever. A few seconds drifted by, then I added, "Your skills are improving."

She scoffed a little but kept smiling. "Maybe so. Still got a lot of learning to do."

"That's entirely true. Ariana's got a lot to teach you. Stick with it."

"I plan to," she said, then paused as if choosing her words. "Which means you'll be seeing more of me." She paused again, still not looking at me. "Maybe a lot more. That okay with you?"

I sighed. The cuffs were gone. The enhancing spell that had pushed my feelings for, well, for everything, had long since dissipated. I felt as calm as ever. Job done, bad guy dispatched, game over. I was perfectly cool and collected.

I turned to face her and found her looking right back at me. She was a mess, dirty and sweat-stained, with a bruise coming in on her forehead, just over her right eye. Her clothes were dusty and ripped, and she was tired as hell. And she was absolutely, one hundred percent beautiful to me. At the sight of her, my insides did the same ridiculous gymnastics as they had before. It hadn't been the cuffs at all. It was just me. Before I could stop myself, I reached up and slowly tucked her hair over her left ear. Dammit, she bit her lip when I did it. Why'd she have to do that?

It took every bit of restraint I had, but I let my hand fall away and I looked straight ahead again.

"Fine by me," I said.

"Okay. Good," she replied. I expected her to be upset or frustrated. She wasn't either. All I felt from her was anticipation. And desire. This was going to be complicated.

But it might also be fun. At that thought, I smiled bigger than I had in a long time.

That's when a pair of bare, scrawny legs appeared before us, knobby knees at our eye level. I frowned and looked up to see Cyrus, fully dressed from the waist up, but wearing only faded boxers and brown dress socks below. He fumed at us, furious.

"Thanks for nothing!" he chided us both. "I've been stuck in the floor over there this whole time. Had to wiggle out of my shoes and trousers to escape. If you don't mind, I need help getting them out of the concrete. I'd just as soon not leave them for the police to find along with,"—he nodded in Malleus's direction—"that." He caught sight of Ariana limping and grimaced. "Oh my! Here, dear, let me look at that foot. I think I can help." Forgetting he was half-naked, Cyrus darted towards her.

I had to chuckle at the old man as I rose to my feet. "Yes, let's get this place cleaned up a little. It'll be light soon, and we need to be out of here before someone gets nosy." I glanced over at Avery and caught her looking at me again. I held her gaze. She didn't look away. She winked at me and turned to check on Ariana and Max.

I had a very distinct feeling that my life was about to be very interesting. And I was right. So very right.

Chapter 19

Max was an enormous help once the dust had settled. I don't know where he found a crew on such short notice, but they arrived not twenty minutes after he borrowed Avery's cell phone. They removed Malleus's corpse and scrubbed the whole place down until no trace of us could be found there. They even got Cyrus's pants and shoes out of the concrete for him, much to his relief. Edge showed up as well, carrying some clothes to cover Max's impressive frame. We gathered behind the empty store as they all finished up. I wore my usual human appearance. I figured Max's crew might know he was a werewolf, but there was a chance they might not. In any case, I saw no need to let them know I was anything other than ordinary.

"Won't the owners have questions when they see all the damage?" Ariana asked Max. He chuckled.

"It's fine. I'm buying the place as-is when the banks open. I'll figure out what to do with it later, but I'm sure the owners will accept my offer without bothering to come take a look at it." He spotted me off to one side. "Here, let me speak to Kane for a bit." Ariana smiled and kissed him on the cheek before ambling over to talk to Avery and Edge.

Max looked tired, but still dapper in his expensive suit. He walked over and stood there beside me for a moment, just smiling. Finally, he spoke. "I'm amused that I feel I owe you my life even though you killed me tonight."

"That was only temporary."

"Yes, and I'm quite glad of that!" Max laughed in that booming musical voice of his. He sobered somewhat, though the smile stayed on his face. "I took a chance trusting you. Grims are known to be logical and goal-driven to a fault. The Fae generally don't lose sleep over one human life, even that of a werewolf. I'd have guessed you'd dispose of me in a heartbeat if it suited you, unfettered by emotions as your kind is reputed to be."

I thought about that. Emotions were, indeed, a real pain. They seemed to cause no end of trouble. Humans seethed with them, while mine seemed quite simple in comparison. Most of the time, anyway. Maybe it was my age, or maybe it was because I spent more time around humans, but I felt different. I realized I'd felt that way for the last few decades or so. Changed, somehow. And if I really thought about it, I'd have to admit that I didn't mind. When I spoke again, I shared the truth.

"Most Grims are exactly like that, yes. Very logical. They'd have just killed you right away. You might not have even seen them coming. Had they been dumb enough to get suckered into an agreement like that one, they'd have done the most logical thing, which was to kill you as quickly as possible to get themselves out of the deal, then kill the bad guy."

Max laughed again. "In a way, that's exactly what you did! But you asked my permission. You told me what you were doing and gave me a fighting chance to survive. My experience with your folk is somewhat limited, but you. . ." he shook his head, "you're unusual among your kind, I'd say."

I shrugged. "I am what I am. I appreciate your trust. I'd probably be handless and magickally crippled right now if you hadn't trusted me."

"True. But he was only using you to get to me. Had he chosen some simpler method, I might be dead of a sniper's bullet right now instead of walking out of here. Because of you, I'm alive." He extended an enormous hand. "Thank you."

I reached out and took it, gave it one firm shake, then let go. "I had a lot of help. Wasn't just me."

He surveyed our little group, smiling widest when his eyes fell on Ariana, who beamed right back at him.

"Indeed. I'm a lucky man."

I smiled. "I agree." I sighed, not happy about what I was about to say next, "Max, Elias Bress was involved in this. He helped Malleus. Gave him information about all of us. That's why Malleus compelled me to kill you. Because of what Ariana and I did to Bress when we helped you escape."

Max growled, caught himself, then sighed. "I worried he'd turn up at some point. He's been remarkably adept at staying hidden. His businesses are all running well, and he's funneling money creatively enough that my people can't trace it. He's been a ghost ever since you two evicted him from here." He turned those amber eyes toward me, "He definitely has a bone to pick with all of us. He's not the forgiving type." He turned away again, catching Ariana's eye from across the parking lot. He smiled in spite of himself, and she smiled back. "I'll put more people on it. We'll find him. Until we do, watch yourself, Kane. And call on me if you need anything at all."

"Will do, your Majesty."

He laughed again. I liked his laugh. "After all we've been through, please, call me Max." The King of the Werewolves slapped me companionably on the back and turned to Ariana and Avery, who were talking with Edge. To Ariana, he said, "Ariana my dear, would you be interested in accompanying me to Dallas for the rest of the week? I feel the need to recuperate from this little adventure and my ranch sounds like just the place. You can shower at my hotel before we leave this afternoon."

She didn't miss a beat. "That sounds like heaven to me." She turned to Avery and said, "Hey, would you mind housesitting for me while I'm away? You can keep working on your lessons in the conjuring room."

Avery nodded. "Oh, sure. I've got the keys to your Jeep, and I'll drive it back to your place. I need to get my car anyway." Avery glanced at me with a tilt of her head. "You can come along if you like, Kane."

I nodded but didn't reply. Words were failing me, and it's always better to be mistaken for a fool than to open your mouth and remove all doubt.

Instead, I watched Cyrus duck into a car with one of Max's people, which then drove away. He, too, had been exhausted from throwing down with Malleus, but I could also feel his satisfaction. He might have been caught by Malleus's trick, but his skills had made it possible to return Ariana to her own body, as well as give us the tools to beat him. He'd more than earned a pat on the back. In addition, having Maximus von Gerhardt owe you one is a pretty big deal, and he knew it. I had no doubt that Cyrus would be touching base with the billionaire at the first opportunity.

I'd known Cyrus for a long time but had never been close to him. No surprise there, I was close to very few people, but I found I liked the little guy. He was feisty. And he had some serious spellcrafting skills. I made a mental note to talk to him about that. He'd taken Avery's buckler back, but left me with the crystal pendant, and I'd begun to wonder if he might have other toys that suited me. My natural gifts were prodigious, but as I'd seen recently, they had their limitations. I also wondered if I should tell him about the little red car that Max and I had trashed at his hotel. If my luck ran true, that had been his, stolen by Malleus while in Ariana's body.

Nah, I'll just let him figure it out, I thought.

The sound of doors slamming brought me out of my musing. The unmarked panel truck that had brought the cleanup crew started up and pulled away, followed directly after by Max's limo. That left Avery and me alone. With each other. Just the two of us. I blinked a few times as I rolled things around in my head. Words, again. They were troublesome things at times.

"Hey," she said, her voice soft and clear.

I turned to regard her, but kept my mouth shut. A stray band of golden light escaped the sunrise and illuminated her face. She tucked a lock of her raven-black hair over her ear, just as I'd done, and a smile played at the corners of her mouth. Standing this close to her, I could sense an awful lot. She was tired, pleased, and excited, all at once. Underlying her emotions was the thread of her magick, like background noise just waiting for the volume to be turned up. She was strong, passionate, and noble, and the light and shadows that played across her face made her look as beautiful as any woman, Fae or human, I'd ever seen. Truthfully, even more so.

My black heart flipped a little. Cuffs or no cuffs, I wanted her, and I wanted her *badly*. But she was human. Humans and Fae don't mix well in the long term. The short term could be fun, but. . .dangerous. For her, especially. If I lost control, I could break her. But it had been a long time. A very, very long time. I stared into those pale, grey-green eyes and let my mind wander. Just a little. And I think she heard me because she blushed.

When she spoke again, her voice had taken on a lower, rougher tone. "I want to ask you something."

I raised an eyebrow. "Yes?"

"Do you...?" She stopped, then started again, "Should we...?" Frustrated, she shook her head and sighed. Then she squared her shoulders and continued. "Are you hungry? I'm hungry. We should go eat somewhere. We should eat *a lot*."

I blinked at her. I've been doing that a lot lately, I know, but it gives me a moment before I say something stupid. I looked away as I considered the idea, bringing one hand to my chin. Deep thinker, that's me.

I turned back to her, admiring this fierce, gorgeous, magickal woman, and chose my words carefully.

"How about tacos? I know a place."

The End

For updates about new releases,
exclusive promotions,
and a complimentary short story,
visit the author's website
and sign up for the VIP mailing list
at
http://www.whitmcclendon.com

The Fire of the Jidaan Trilogy Boxset

Epic Fantasy that will sweep you away...

"...a truly imaginative trio of books..."

"...hard to put down...I was on the edge of my seat!"

Reyanna's Prophecy
Book 1 of the Forge Born Duology

The adventure continues...

"...an engaging, exciting and action-packed fantasy adventure, well-crafted...a welcome sense of humour as well..."

About the Author

Whit McClendon was born on October 31, 1969 in Freeport, Tx. He grew up in Angleton, Texas and was active in martial arts, track and field, and he played the clarinet in band. One year at TX A & M proved that lacrosse was far more fun than electrical engineering, and he eventually graduated with a degree in Engineering Design Graphics from Brazosport College. After working in the petrochemical field as a CAD drafter for many years, Whit finally realized his life's dream of becoming a full-time martial arts instructor. He now lives in Katy, Texas, plays lacrosse as often as possible, and runs Jade Mountain Martial Arts. He laughs a lot more now than he did when he worked at the engineering firm.

whitmcc@jidaan.com
www.whitmcclendon.com
www.jmma.org